Happy St. Patrick's Day 2010 Nick!

Love,
Grom and Pa

FOLKTALES OF THE WORLD

The King with Horse's Ears

AND OTHER IRISH FOLKTALES

FOLKTALES OF THE WORLD

RETOLD BY
Batt Burns

ILLUSTRATED BY
Igor Oleynikov

STERLING

New York / London
www.sterlingpublishing.com/kids

To my great wife and friend, Maura, and to my grandchildren, Aisling, Laoise, and Robert.

STERLING and the distinctive Sterling logo are registered trademarks of Sterling Publishing Co., Inc.

Library of Congress Cataloging-in-Publication Data

Burns, Batt.
  The king with horse's ears and other Irish folktales / Batt Burns.
     p. cm.
   Contents: The king with horse's ears - Fionn Mac Cumhail and the Fianna of Ireland - The greedy barber - The charm setter - A famous thief - Back from the fairies - Oisin in the Land of the Ever Young - Just one choice - Paying the rent -The boy and the Pooka - A strange night - A clever leprechaun - The Lost Island of Lonesome Seals.
   ISBN 978-1-4027-3772-5
  1. Fairy tales-Ireland. 2. Tales-Ireland. [1. Fairy tales. 2. Folklore-Ireland.] I. Title.
  PZ8.B94Ki 2009
   [398.2]-dc22   2007035258

10 9 8 7 6 5 4 3 2 1

Published by Sterling Publishing Co., Inc.
387 Park Avenue South, New York, NY 10016
Text © 2009 by Batt Burns
Illustrations © 2009 by Igor Oleynikov
The artwork for this book was created in gouache, then finished digitally.
Distributed in Canada by Sterling Publishing
ᶜ/o Canadian Manda Group, 165 Dufferin Street
Toronto, Ontario, Canada M6K 3H6
Distributed in the United Kingdom by GMC Distribution Services
Castle Place, 166 High Street, Lewes, East Sussex, England BN7 1XU
Distributed in Australia by Capricorn Link (Australia) Pty. Ltd.
P.O. Box 704, Windsor, NSW 2756, Australia

Printed in China
All rights reserved

Sterling ISBN 978-1-4027-3772-5

For information about custom editions, special sales, premium and corporate purchases, please contact Sterling Special Sales Department at 800-805-5489 or specialsales@sterlingpublishing.com.

Designed by Lauren Rille

CONTENTS

Note: Because of their Gaelic origins, some of the words in this book may be unfamiliar to you and difficult to pronounce. Toward the end of the book, you will find a Glossary that includes the definition and pronunciation of many Gaelic words. If the pronunciation is not in the Glossary, it will be footnoted within the story itself. Most of the Gaelic words not in the Glossary are names of characters or places.

INTRODUCTION

I was fortunate to have first experienced the magic world of Irish storytelling at a young age. I was born in the remote village of Sneem, nestled at the foot of Macgillycuddy's Reeks, a high, craggy mountain range that forms the backbone of the Iveragh Peninsula in County Kerry.

Four miles east of my home village lived my grandfather, Michael Clifford (b. 1875). He was a good storyteller in the traditional seanachie mold, and had lived the life of a typical small farmer, which had changed very little from the late nineteenth century. My grandmother, who gave birth to twelve children, saw most of them emigrate to North America and England, for there was no future for them in the impoverished Ireland of those days.

I stepped into the world of my grandparents when I was about four years of age and spent extended periods with them over the next seven years. Here, I experienced first-hand the dying remnants of ancient Irish customs, folklore, traditions, and farming methods. There was a strong residue of the Gaelic language in the English spoken in that district, and my grandfather's stories were laced with Gaelic phrases.

During the time I have been writing this book of folktales, vivid and enduring memories of those magical, far-off days have come flooding back. These include listening to my grandfather tell great stories on stormy winter nights while seated by the open hearth, where a blazing fire of peat and logs raged in defiance at the howling Atlantic gales. Here, I rode with Oisin and Niamh to the magical land of Tir na nOg and wondered if Fionn Mac Cumhail would be able to overcome the King of the World in single combat at the Battle of Ventry. I remember shaking with fear as I ascended the stairs to bed with a candle, having listened to my grandfather's tale of the Black Pooka. Many nights I pleaded for more stories about "the Liberator," Daniel O'Connell, for I loved the ingenious way in which he could get poor people out of trouble.

Radio and TV had not found a place in that country farmhouse, and there was lots of time for conversation. There was magic even in the physical landscape of my grandparents' infertile farm. The large rock visible from the front door of their humble home had been tossed there in a fit of anger by the great hero Cuchulainn when he was up on Slieve Mish about fifty miles away! I used to walk through the earthen fairy fort of Lissaree on my way to school, but did not dare go near it after dark, because the Wee Folk, or fairies, often tried to lure in children, whom they could train to be warriors in Fairyland. I was warned never to break off any branches of the lone blackthorn tree, sacred to the fairies, which stood just beyond

seanachie (*Shan-ock-kee*); Oisin (*Uh-sheen*); Niamh (*Nee-ahv*); Tir na nOg (*Tier neh Knowg*); Fionn Mac Cumhail (*Fewn Mock Cool*) the eastern gable of the house. According to my grandfather, an ancestor of mine had failed to heed that warning and ended up with a withered hand. Is it any wonder that today I have a healthy respect for the "other world" of the Wee Folk!

My purpose in writing this book is to re-create for you a little of the fascination and magic that I was privileged to experience as a child. Reading or listening to stories takes us on flights of fancy away from our troubles and worries, and powers our imaginations.

When selecting tales, I had an extensive well of material from which to draw. Storytelling is Ireland's oldest tradition and, fortunately, thousands of tales have been written down and preserved in ancient manuscripts since the early Christian era of the fifth century. Great collectors of tales like Thomas Croker, Thomas Keightley, William Carleton, and Samuel Lover did invaluable work in the early nineteenth century, and in the latter part of the same century Lady Augusta Gregory, Lady Wilde, Standish O'Grady, and Douglas Hyde preserved many tales that would otherwise have vanished from memory. Ireland's famous poet W. B. Yeats drew much inspiration for his early poetry from his own large collection of folktales.

Some stories in my collection—"Oisin in the Land of the Ever Young" and "Fionn Mac Cumhail and the Fianna of Ireland"—are retellings of well-known ancient tales that I first heard from my mother, Margaret Burns. I have also included a number of new stories that were inspired by great local tellers from my youth. One of these seanachies, Tady Pad O'Sullivan, worked for my father, and was unable to read or write. But he more than made up for that by the richness of his imagination and expression in the oral tradition. It was one of his stories from more than fifty years ago that inspired the tale "Paying the Rent." Tady had the rare gift of composing tales as he went along and was in big demand around Sneem firesides. If the Good Lord had given me that wonderful gift, you would not have had to wait until now for my first book of Irish folktales!

Over the past twenty years, it has been my privilege to share many of these stories with children all over my own country as well as throughout the United States. My greatest reward has been to see the radiant light of wonder shine in the eyes of my audiences.

It is my dearest wish that this book will provide you with enjoyable reading and that it will also give you an insight into the rich culture and traditions of my country. I hope that it will trigger a desire in you to read more collections of Irish tales—and, who knows, one day, like me, you may even become a seanachie yourself!

Cuchulainn (*Coo-kullin*); Slieve (*Shlee-ahv*)

BACK FROM THE FAIRIES

Fairies, like mortals, often have serious misunderstandings and disagreements. Large groups fight battles near fairy forts and on remote hillsides after midnight. Some groups seek the help of mortals, who are so much stronger than fairies, and kidnap baby boys to fight in the wars when they grow up. In the boys' places are left changelings, creatures with fiery eyes and puckered features who scream and whine continuously. To lose their only child to the Wee Folk seemed a real possibility for Kate and Larry until they discovered an important secret.

Life was tough for the poor sheep farmers who struggled to make a living on the rocky foothills of Macgillycuddy's Reeks, and Larry O'Shea was no exception. He and his wife of ten years, Kate, lived in a one-room thatched cottage that overlooked the fairy fort of Lissaree, a place where, according to old people, a lot of otherwordly activity went on in the darkness of the long winter nights. Few dared to pass the fort after midnight, lest they be lured in by the haunting music or be tempted to join in the revelry of the Wee Folk.

More than anything else, Kate and Larry longed for a child of their very own, but it seemed that the Good Lord was not going to bless them with such a wonderful gift. Like all of their neighbors, Kate and Larry went to the holy well of Saint Crohane on July 29, the saint's feast day, and prayed fervently as they circled the well numerous times. Six months later, Kate knew that she was going to be a mother. When the baby was eventually born in early September, the couple's joy knew no bounds. They guarded their bouncing baby boy like gold dust. Each evening when Larry returned from the hill, they would sit on either side of the cradle and dote on their beautiful child.

One dark, dreary night in the depths of winter, Kate was suddenly awoken from her sleep by the loud howling of the wind outside. Her husband lay snoring beside her. He was unusually tired on that particular night, having spent most of the day on the hill searching for two of his sheep. A tiny flame from a dying ember of burning peat flickered in the hearth and illuminated the sleeping face of the baby in the cradle at the foot of the bed.

All of a sudden, the bolted kitchen door opened with a menacing creak. The swirling wind blew the remaining embers in the hearth to life, revealing two dark, ominous figures standing in the doorway. Kate tried to scream, but she was so paralyzed with fear that no words left her mouth. At the door stood the hooded figure of an old hag with a twisted mouth and fiery eyes. Right behind her, bearing a sickly, misshapen child in her arms, was a second hag with tousled hair and eyes like coals of fire. The ugly pair moved toward the hearth and warmed themselves. Then the hooded hag turned her fiery gaze on the cradle. A flash of lightning revealed fairy faces at the windows outside. Kate saw the hag move toward the cradle and fainted.

When she recovered from her fainting spell, Kate woke her husband with a piercing scream. Grabbing him, she shouted at him to light a candle. As soon as he did, the flame was blown out by one of the hags, who was still lurking in the darkness. As the candle was blown out a second time, a series of thunderclaps tore through the night sky. Larry and Kate could hear peals of hollow, mocking laughter inside and outside the house.

Larry flew into a black rage. He leaped from the bed and grabbed the tongs from the fire to strike the hag. As he raised his hand, he felt the full force of a blackthorn stick on the back of his head. Now his fury knew no bounds. He quickly opened the kitchen door, grabbed the hag, and threw her out into the howling gale.

He was hardly able to breathe as he banged the door shut and waited for Kate to relight the candle. When she did and they looked in the cradle, they saw a hideous little imp with hair growing all over its face. Their heart-rending cries almost shattered the walls of their humble abode and were carried by the howling winds into the neighboring towns.

Suddenly, as if from nowhere, a tiny woman with a red necktie appeared in front of them. "What is the cause of your wailing and screaming at this unearthly hour of the night when all of the world is asleep?" she asked.

"Take one look at the cradle yonder and you will see the cause of our cries," roared Larry, who couldn't control his anger and his grief. Kate, who was a little calmer, told the woman everything that had happened.

The strange visitor rushed to the cradle, grabbed the baby, and hugged it, as tears of joy streamed down her face. "How can you look so happy in the midst of our tragedy and terrible loss?" barked Larry, who was beginning to boil over with anger again.

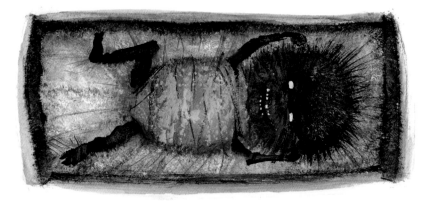

"I'll tell you," answered the stranger forcefully. "This is my child, who was taken from me earlier tonight. I am one of the fairy folk of Lissaree. My people have admired your son ever since he was born. They tried to steal him on two previous occasions, for they want him to fight in the fairy wars when he gets older. Tonight they succeeded in replacing your child with mine. Even though this child looks ugly and misshapen to you, to me he is the most beautiful child ever born. I understand the grief of losing a child, and I will let you in on the secret of how to get your son back."

Larry and Kate moved closer to the fairy woman. "One week from now, on November Eve, a great gathering of our people will take place at Staigue Fort, several miles west of here. It is one of our biggest feasts of the year. Lissaree will be unguarded, apart from the two nursemaids who will be left behind to watch over your child. Like all of the fairies, they are scared of fire because they do not have the power to extinguish it. Go there after midnight with a sheaf of corn and a flame," the fairy woman said. "Tell the nurses that you will set fire to the fort if they do not return your child." Then, with a flash of lightning that almost blinded Larry and Kate, she was gone.

On November Eve, Larry took a flaming torch and a sheaf of corn to the ancient fort. As he stood at the entrance and lit the sheaf, he heard a woman scream inside. Almost immediately, two fairy women appeared in utter panic. Before they had time to speak, Larry said, "I want my son back, or I'll burn every tree and bush around this fort, even your chambers underneath, so that your people will be homeless."

"Stay your hand, stay your hand," the fairies cried. "We cannot stand the power of fire and corn. You can have your child back."

Instantly, one of the women rushed back into the fort and reappeared with the baby. "Take him," she said. "Now that he is yours, listen well to my advice. When you put him in the cradle tonight, take a glowing cinder from the fire and circle the cradle three times. No more will fairy power be able to reach him."

Larry did as he was instructed, and from that night on, his beautiful baby boy was nevermore troubled by the fairy folk of Lissaree. But he would not risk bringing on the anger of the fairies, and so Larry protected the fort. He never allowed anybody to cut a single tree or bush, or interfere with the ancient site in any way.

And so, after midnight, all through the winter, the fairy folk of Lissaree still sing, dance, and make merry to the music of the fairy pipes, just as their ancestors have done for thousands of years, and like their ancestors will do for generations to come.

THE KING WITH HORSE'S EARS

The strange story of King Labhraidh Loingseach and his mysterious secret has been a favorite around Irish firesides for hundreds of years. Fearful of how his people will react to his secret, the king kills anyone who discovers the truth. But when he confides in a barber named Johnny Gruagach, King Labhraidh learns that keeping a secret isn't always best and that it is important to be able to laugh at yourself.

King Labhraidh Loingseach was a proud king, and very sensitive about the way he looked. His royal cloak was sewn in twenty different colors and was held together at the neck by a gold Tara brooch, and the unusual crown on his head was studded with diamonds from a distant land. The king's crown was designed in such a way that a light piece of gold-plated metal hung down at each side of his head to cover his ears. His auburn beard was always trimmed to perfection, and nothing pleased him more than to be the center of attention at the many banquets and feasts that he attended all over the country.

But this well-known king harbored a dark secret. He had been born with horse's ears! His crown ensured that nobody would discover his embarrassing secret. In fact, the queen was the only person in the whole kingdom who knew it. She had discovered the king's ears when he took off his crown on their wedding night. Right then he had made her promise that she would never reveal his secret to anyone.

Just like everybody else, the king had to have a haircut every five or six weeks. A barber from somewhere in his kingdom was always selected at random, brought to the palace, and ordered to cut the king's hair. On completion of the haircut, the unfortunate barber was taken into the dungeon and killed. King Labhraidh was taking no chances.

Labhraidh Loingseach (*Louw-ree Leen-shock*)

When news of these disappearances spread, all of the barbers went into hiding. Not one could be found to give the king a haircut. His hair grew extremely long, and he became more embarrassed and angry with each passing day.

Early one morning, the king called in two of his trusted soldiers and ordered them to get their horses ready. "Before darkness falls tomorrow night, I want you to provide me with a barber," he told them. "And no more of this nonsense that one cannot be found."

As they left the courtyard on their horses, the soldiers knew that the king was very serious. It would not be wise to return without fulfilling his order.

On the first day, they had no luck. But things changed early the next morning when they came into a remote village in the mountains. Young Johnny Gruagach, who lived with his widowed mother, had just drawn back the bolt on the front door of his barbershop when the two soldiers grabbed him, tied his hands behind his back, and told him that it was his turn to give King Labhraidh a haircut. As they marched him off to the palace, Johnny knew that his fate was sealed, but still he begged and pleaded with them to release him and find another barber.

"We're under orders from the king. It's your life or ours," barked one of the men.

The guards were about halfway to the castle when Johnny's mother finished her breakfast and entered her son's barbershop for a chat. To her surprise, it was empty and the front door was wide open. Suddenly a neighbor rushed through the door almost completely out of breath.

"They have taken your son to the palace to give the king a haircut," she gushed in alarm.

"What?" screamed the widow as the reality of her son's situation flashed across her mind. She became so distraught that her cries could be heard all over the village.

Eventually she was calmed by kindly neighbors and vowed that she would neither eat nor sleep until she pleaded with the king himself for her son's life. She began the long trek to the palace and succeeded in getting to the room where the king sat on his throne. Throwing herself on the floor in front of him, she looked up with pleading, tear-filled eyes.

"Johnny is all I have in the world, Your Majesty. My husband died when our son was a baby. The little that Johnny earns from barbering keeps us from starving. Please, don't kill him. We will do anything you want. Anything."

The king was moved and did not speak for some time. "My good woman," he finally said, "you have put me in an impossible position. Your pleas would soften a heart of stone, but how can I trust an unknown barber with a profound personal secret? Can you answer me that?"

"May the Lord strike me dead if my son doesn't keep the darkest secret that Your Majesty could tell," sobbed the old woman.

The king stood up from his throne before he spoke and looked gravely at the widow. "Very soon your son will give me a haircut in a room at the back of the castle. There he will discover a secret. If he ever reveals it to a living being, both of your lives will be ended. Now go back to your village. Your son's life will be spared." The poor woman was overcome with joy and repeatedly thanked the king.

A short time later, her terrified son was led to a small room just beyond the banquet hall where the king sat in readiness. "Bolt that door and close those window shutters," he ordered sharply. A tall candle had already been lit, and Johnny began by removing the crown from the king's head. To his utter astonishment, up popped two horse's ears that almost hit him in the face! Despite his terror, Johnny almost laughed at the incredible sight before his eyes, but he was able to hold it in. In total silence and showing no reaction, the barber completed his task.

"Young man, let me give you one of the sternest warnings that I have ever given in my life," said the king. "Your life is being spared on the condition that you never breathe a word to anybody about what you saw here today. If you do, not one more day will dawn for you."

And so the happiest barber in Ireland left the palace of King Labhraidh Loingseach and, in a state of high elation, returned to his own village, where everybody wondered how he had escaped with his life. Many people tried to coax information out of him, but he remained faithful to his promise. As the days passed, the longing to share his secret became stronger and stronger. He felt as if it were going to overpower him. Soon he was unable to eat his food, and he grew sick and weak.

When his mother eventually called the doctor, he was baffled by the barber's complaint. A thorough examination revealed no illness. "Are you just pretending to be sick?" asked the doctor quizzically. The barber reassured him that this was not the case. "Is there anything troubling your mind?" inquired the doctor, looking hopeful.

"I have a secret that I am bursting to tell, but I cannot tell it," came the quick answer.

The doctor informed him that if he did not unload his secret fairly soon, he might not be around to do it, for he could die.

"If I tell the secret to a single person, the king will have my life. I am caught both ways," moaned the barber.

The doctor stroked his long grey beard and thought long and hard before he spoke next. "I know that you are feeling weak and tired, but you must make a special effort to get out of bed tomorrow morning and go to the Wood of Direen. Find the tallest oak tree at the right side of the track that leads into the wood. Walk up to it and tell your secret to its trunk. This will allow you to relieve yourself of the secret without breaking your promise."

The barber followed the doctor's instructions and whispered these words to the tree: "King Labhraidh Loingseach has two horse's ears." As soon as he said this, all the pain and anguish left his body and went straight into the tree. He rushed back home in great form.

"I can't believe it!" said his mother in amazement. "You were hardly able to walk when you left here an hour ago. What happened in the forest?" Johnny was just about to answer when he remembered his promise and thought better of it.

A month later, the king hosted a big feast to celebrate a great harvest. All of the neighboring royalty was invited, as well as many poets and musicians. The chief entertainer would be Fintan, the king's famous harpist, who always liked to rehearse for a long period on the day of a performance. But when he opened his harp case on the morning of the feast, he discovered that the timber at the base had cracked and several strings were hanging loosely. It would have to be repaired as soon as possible.

Fintan rushed out to a shed at the back of the castle, grabbed a saw, and saddled his horse. He dismounted at the Wood of Direen and cut a suitable piece of timber off an oak tree. Little did he know that it was to this very tree that the barber had told his secret. Instead of rehearsing, Fintan spent the day repairing his harp and arrived in the banquet hall just as King Labhraidh was addressing the assembly.

"Noble guests, you have honored me with your presence here tonight for the celebration of a bountiful harvest. It is now my great pleasure to call on Fintan, the prince of harpers, to entertain you all."

The cloaked figure of a bearded harpist emerged from a room beside the banquet hall. He stepped onto a little raised platform and put his harp in its place. There was a hush as Fintan gently stroked the strings. Suddenly, to the utter dismay of all, including Fintan, these words rang out and continued to be repeated: "King Labhraidh Loingseach has two horse's ears."

The king, who had turned pale, glared at Fintan. The harpist's eyes bore a terrified look. A giggle or two was heard from a table at the rear of the hall. Soon the sporadic giggles became a river of laughter. King Labhraidh Loingseach was now boiling over with rage, as he realized that his secret was out. But the laughter in the hall was increasing. A smile inched its way across the king's lips, and without warning, he lifted the crown from his head, revealing the huge ears. The rollicking laughter almost lifted the roof off the banquet hall.

From that day forward, not another barber was killed in the green land of Ireland. And as for Johnny Gruagach, he became the resident barber at the palace, with the distinction of giving haircuts to many noble kings and princes from all over Ireland.

FIONN MAC CUMHAIL
AND THE FIANNA OF IRELAND

The Fianna were a legendary band of warriors who guarded Ireland from foreign invaders in ancient times. They were famous for their courage and for being faithful to their promises, but above all, the Fianna were famous for their strength. Only the bravest and wisest men were allowed membership in this elite group. This story introduces Fionn, the most famous of all Fianna warriors, whose heroic deeds have fascinated young and old around Irish firesides for centuries.

Of all the high kings of Ireland who graced the regal mansions of Tara in County Meath, few could match Cormac Mac Airt in wisdom, bravery, or leadership. King Cormac saw the need for an elite band of warriors to guard the coast of Ireland, and he formed the Fianna. He estimated that he would need at least fifteen thousand men to carry out tasks such as protecting him, upholding his laws, ensuring that tribute was promptly paid by all chieftains, and making certain that his enemies could never plot his overthrow.

"Anyone wishing to join the Fianna must be wise, exemplary in conduct, strong in limb, powerful and skilled in battle, and well versed in the folklore and poetry of Ireland," announced King Cormac at one of the great fairs of Tara in the month of August. He then called forward his chief advisor, who listed the outlandish skills necessary for membership.

"Each warrior must be able to leap over a stick as high as his head and bend under a tree branch at the height of his knee without touching his hands to the ground," began the advisor in a pretentious voice. "Standing alone in a hole three feet deep, and using only his shield and a hazel rod for protection, he must be

---

Fionn Mac Cumhail (*Fewn Mock Cool*); Fianna (*Fee-ah-na*); Cormac Mac Airt (*Kur-mock Mock Art*)

able to defend himself from nine men casting spears at him. If a warrior is not sufficiently light-footed to run through the forest in October without breaking any of the withered twigs on the ground, then he is not fit to join the Fianna."

The chief advisor listed many more skills, including extracting a thorn from the sole of the foot without breaking stride as one ran through the countryside, swimming upriver against a strong current for three hours, and knowing at least twelve books of poetry by heart. When he was finished, he said, "Purity in our hearts, strength in our limbs, and action based on our promises—this will be the motto of King Cormac's Fianna." And so the Fianna came to be.

Fionn Mac Cumhail was not the first leader of the Fianna, but he was the most famous. Fionn was just a boy when his father was killed. The high king had selected Fionn's father, Cumhal, as the first leader of the Fianna because of his knowledge of magical arts, his great strength, his courage, and his trustworthiness. But the sons of Goll Mac Morna, a member of the Fianna, were very jealous and thought their own father should have been chosen. Unable to gain their loyalty, Cumhal used his magical power to exile them, some to Scotland, some to Greece, and some to the Northlands of Norway and Sweden. The men were deeply upset at being banished and separated from one another. And so after an absence of sixteen years, they returned to Ireland and killed Cumhal.

Fionn's life was now in danger as well, and he was taken into hiding in the Slieve Bloom Mountains. There, he lived for ten years, while two old women trained him in all the skills of battle. He then spent seven years with Finnegas, a poet and seer who lived beside the River Boyne.

For many years, Finnegas had sought without success to capture the Salmon of Knowledge from the river. Early on a glorious May morning, Fionn was roused from his sleep by shouts of joy from the riverbank. Finnegas, who had been up

---

Cumhal (*Cool*); Goll Mac Morna (*Goul Mock Mor-na*); Slieve (*Shlee-ahv*); Finnegas (*Fin-neh-gas*)

since dawn, had finally captured the elusive salmon and was in a rapturous mood.

"Come, young man. Prepare the fire and put this fish to roast on the spit," he ordered. "I cannot wait to get my first taste, for at that moment all knowledge of future events will be mine."

The old man laughed uncontrollably and then stretched out on the grassy bank to watch Fionn prepare the fire. Soon his eyelids began to drop. The excitement had been too much for him and he needed to rest. Just before he fell asleep, he issued a warning to Fionn: "It has been my life's ambition to capture that fish. Whatever you do, make sure that you do not burn it. And most importantly, do not take a bite of it before I do."

Some time later, Fionn became alarmed when he noticed a blister rise on the back of the fish. He had delayed too long before turning it on the spit!

Instinctively, he pressed the blister with his thumb, but the sharp pain caused by the searing heat forced him to stick his thumb in his mouth. At that very moment, Finnegas awoke. He immediately noticed something strange about Fionn, who bore a bewildered look.

"Are you feeling all right?" asked the old man, a little alarmed.

Fionn said that thoughts and images of future times were swirling around in his head. A vivid picture in his brain showed himself at the head of a band of several hundred soldiers on their way to the court of King Cormac Mac Airt at Tara.

"You have eaten of the Salmon of Knowledge and broken your promise!" shouted Finnegas in dismay. He covered his eyes with his hands so that Fionn would not notice his tears.

"No, no, I haven't," pleaded Fionn earnestly. Then he remembered putting his thumb on the blister.

But Finnegas bore no ill will toward Fionn for having the first taste of the fish and told him that his Thumb of Knowledge would serve him well when he became the leader of the Fianna. "All you will have to do is to put your thumb in your mouth, and you will immediately be filled with the information you seek," said the old man. "I was too old to receive such a gift anyway, but you will put it to good use and it will save you from much misfortune."

At last the time came for Fionn to leave Finnegas. With the skills and knowledge he had acquired in the Slieve Bloom Mountains and on the River Boyne, the warrior presented himself at King Cormac's court to claim his place in the Fianna. His father, Cumhal, had been greatly respected by King Cormac, and the king agreed to admit his son to the Fianna. Soon Fionn was in charge of a distinguished band of warriors. Among his men were the great runner, Caoilte Mac Ronain, who in the course of one day could run from one end of Ireland to the other,

---

Caoilte Mac Ronain (*Keel-tah Mock Row-nawn*)

and Diarmaid O'Duibhne, who had a spot on his forehead that caused every woman he met to fall madly in love with him.

Fionn was extremely handsome and needed no such spot to make the young women want to marry him. One evening as he returned from a hunt along a wooded slope of the Hill of Allen, his faithful dogs, Bran and Sceolan, disturbed a young fawn. The fawn led them on a merry chase through a nearby valley. As the dogs were gaining on the fawn, it suddenly stopped and lay down on a grassy knoll. When Fionn eventually reached the spot, he was met with an extraordinary sight. The dogs had not killed the fawn, but were playfully licking the face and neck of the beautiful animal. Every now and then, they turned to their master with questioning looks.

"By my word," said Fionn, looking at his dogs, "I never saw you two treat your prey so gently!"

As Fionn headed home, the dogs and the fawn walked along behind him. This was certainly a mystery.

Later that evening, as Fionn sat down to a meal with three of his warriors, the door opened. A beautiful maiden dressed like a princess entered the room and stood across the table from Fionn.

"I am the fawn that your dogs treated so gently today. I refused to marry the Dark Druid some years ago, and he changed me into a wild deer and condemned me to be hunted until I reached the Hill of Allen. Your wonderful dogs recognized that I wasn't a real deer and did not harm me."

Fionn was entranced by this woman's beauty and the sweetness of her voice. He bade her take a seat, and the three warriors left the room with smiles. The maiden's name was Sive, and she and Fionn talked and talked until the first faint light of dawn eased through the large windows. Fionn soon fell in love with Sive

Diarmaid O'Duibhne (*Dear-mad Oh Thee-nah*); Sceolan (*Shk-gow-lan*); Sive (*Sigh-ev*)

and they had a son: the famous warrior, Oisin. The boy was Fionn's pride and joy. At the age of twelve, Oisin was sent to study for two years with Fionn's cousin, where he learned all the skills of arms and horsemanship.

Years later, Oisin fought with his father in the most famous battle of Fionn's life. Dara Donn, the King of the World, accompanied by kings from Greece and

France, had set sail for Ireland with a huge fleet of ships and arrived in Ventry harbor in the southwest.

The kings wished to conquer the whole country and make its residents pay them a tribute of gold, silver, and cattle. Fionn defended Ireland with the best warriors of the Fianna, and after a fierce and bloody conflict that lasted for a year and a day, Fionn and Dara Donn prepared to fight in single combat.

———————
Oisin (*Uh-sheen*); Dara Donn (*Dah-reh Down*)

On the day before the final showdown, Fionn discovered that his opponent could only be wounded by a magical sword that lay hidden in the palace of the King of the Fair Men, far away from Ireland. Fortunately for Fionn, his uncle, Labhran of the Long Hand, had the power to change himself into an eagle and travel with the speed of the wind. There was little time to spare by the time Labhran arrived back with the deadly weapon.

As the two great leaders approached each other to fight, Dara Donn recognized the sword. The great fear he now experienced caused him to fight Fionn with greater ferocity. Many serious wounds were suffered by both combatants, and for a time it looked as if Fionn would fall. As dusk descended on the beach of Ventry harbor, a loud shout of encouragement for Fionn was heard from the Fianna. He lunged forward at Dara with the magic sword and delivered a mortal wound. A great cry of anguish was heard from the foreigners, and before the night was over their ships had set sail for home. Once more, Ireland had been saved from invaders by the Fianna.

Many years later, Fionn fought another famous battle, the Battle of Gabhra, in which he lost his favorite grandson and the Fianna was disbanded. Fionn was by this time well advanced in years, and although he escaped the battle with his life, a deep melancholy came over him. He went into hiding for fear of being captured by the high king, Cairbreh, who believed that the members of the Fianna were too proud and selfish, and demanded too many riches. The warrior Fionn was never seen again. Nobody is sure how or even when his life ended, but some old storytellers say that he lived on for hundreds of years in the form of great Irish heroes.

Labhran (*Louw-raun*); Cairbreh (*Core-ih-breh*)

THE GREEDY BARBER

Daniel O'Connell, also known as "the Liberator," was a famous lawyer. Poor peasants who could not afford lawyers' fees often paid him a visit to seek his advice. All were assured of a fair hearing, expert counseling, and the best hospitality. When Paddy the Bog encountered a devious barber, there was only one man who could possibly help him. Daniel's clever plan not only solved Paddy the Bog's problem, but reminds us that it does not pay to be dishonest.

Paddy the Bog was a legendary turf cutter on the Iveragh Peninsula in the early part of the nineteenth century. It was well known that he could cut as much turf in two days as another man would cut in a week. This came in handy, as turf was widely used to kindle fires in the hearth. Much of Paddy's tiny farm consisted of bogland, and he decided that he could make some badly needed extra money by selling turf to residents of the village of Sneem.

A skilled local basket maker provided Paddy with two spacious baskets made from strong hazel rods, and he purchased a straddle from the harness maker. Too poor to own a horse, Paddy the Bog had a strong donkey that was well able to travel in the soft bogland. The two baskets hung down at each side of the donkey and were tied together with a short piece of rope that crossed over the straddle, which sat in the center of the animal's back.

During the month of September, Paddy the Bog became a familiar sight in the village as he delivered turf to many households. On one particular evening, he was very happy with the one pound and five shillings he collected from five different houses. The five shillings would pay off a bill owed to a local shopkeeper, and he would still have plenty of money left over to buy half a sack of flour to keep his family in bread for another three weeks.

For the first time in several months, he had a few extra shillings and decided that he could afford to spend one shilling on a long overdue haircut. When he arrived at the village barbershop, he was surprised to find that the barber had recently retired due to ill health. He felt a little uncomfortable trying to make conversation with the barber's young son, who had been an apprentice to a barber in the big city of Dublin for more than a year.

Paddy the Bog looked like a new man as he stood up from the barber's chair, dusted off a few loose hairs from his shoulders, and admired himself in the mirror.

"What will I be giving you?" he inquired of the young man.

"That will be one pound," came the quick answer.

Paddy the Bog almost staggered with the shock and was speechless for a full minute.

"Are you out of your mind? A pound for a haircut! Daylight robbery!" barked Paddy the Bog. "If your father were here, he would give me ten haircuts for that price!"

"But my father isn't here anymore," the young barber replied sharply. "Now pay me my money, or you will rue the day you crossed me." Paddy the Bog had no choice except to pay up, but as he left the barbershop he vowed vengeance on the greedy upstart.

As luck would have it, later that evening the famous Daniel O'Connell galloped his horse into the village on his return from a hunt up a nearby hill. As he chatted with a few local men, he was called aside by Paddy the Bog, who was still seething with anger from his earlier experience.

O'Connell, who hadn't shaved for a few days, listened with his usual patience while his mind worked overtime. Before Paddy the Bog had finished his story, Daniel focused his eyes on the donkey standing beside him and he broke into a devilish laugh.

"I want you to tie both my horse and your donkey to that gate on the far side of the street and come with me to the draper's shop," said O'Connell.

Inside the shop, he ordered the draper to loan Paddy the Bog a long black cape and a new hat. To complete the disguise, O'Connell gave him a pair of glasses, which he always kept in his hunting jacket.

As both men made their way to the barbershop, Paddy the Bog tried to keep from laughing at Daniel O'Connell's plan. The famous lawyer was immediately recognized and welcomed heartily by the young barber. Acknowledging the welcome, he said that he was in a big hurry but would like a shave for himself and his companion. Then Daniel and the barber agreed on a price of two shillings for each shave.

Assuming that his companion was the man in the black cape, the barber began to shave Daniel O'Connell. When he had completed his task, the barber called over the man who was seated by the window with his head bent downward.

"No, no," said O'Connell, "that's not him. My companion is still down the street, but this gentleman will call him up."

Paddy the Bog quickly left and within minutes was back in the barbershop with his donkey. Here, he discarded his cape, coat, hat, and glasses. The young barber bore a bewildered look.

"Now," said O'Connell, "start shaving my companion as you promised, and do a good clean job for two shillings!"

"I can't shave a donkey. All of the razors in Ireland wouldn't shave that hairy animal," insisted the young barber.

"Then you have broken your promise to shave my companion, and I will not leave this spot until you place one pound in my hand," came Daniel O'Connell's sharp retort.

The barber knew that he was tricked, and with great reluctance handed over the money, which O'Connell immediately transferred to Paddy the Bog.

The two men laughed heartily as they walked down the village street to return the clothing to the draper, for whom O'Connell had done a favor a year previously. Then, having thanked Daniel O'Connell profusely, Paddy the Bog headed home with a great story for his wife and kids.

THE CHARM SETTER

The idea of a charm setter in Irish culture is one that has given rise to much fear. According to legend, a charm setter could use rituals and incantations to make your crops fail and ensure your cows would stop giving milk. Much of this activity grew out of jealousy and hatred, and occurred on the morning of May Day. One way to avoid becoming the target of a charm setter was to prevent anything from being removed from your house on May Day morning, for with it might go all of your good luck for the coming year. When Honest Bill and his wife suddenly begin to suffer great misfortune, they learn that jealousy is indeed a powerful weapon and that friendship is not always what it seems.

The beginning of summer in Ireland on the first of May was a superstitious time for the remote coastal town of County Mayo. It was a date laden with magic, superstition, custom, and the working of evil charms. It was the latter that was most feared in this particular part of Ireland.

On any other day of the year, shortly after dawn, you would notice blue peat smoke rising from the chimneys of the many thatched cottages of this close-knit farming community. But on May Day morning, the tradition of Codhladh Bealtaine, or May Day Sleep, ensured that the families of this Gaelic-speaking community slept late, for no one wanted to be the first to light a fire. There were no eggs or tea for breakfast, as this would involve lighting a fire to boil water. It was firmly believed that within the community was at least one female charm setter who, by means of incantations and certain hand movements, could draw smoke toward her cottage from a neighbor's chimney and with it bring most of that farmer's supply of butter for the next year. The sale of butter to shopkeepers in town was an important way for housewives to make some extra money.

Codhladh Bealtaine (*Cull-ah Be-owl-tin-eh*)

Sheila Bawn was one such housewife. Sheila had been widowed within six months of her wedding, when her husband had died after a fall from his horse. Sheila's small farm provided grass for only four cows, but within a year of her husband's death, the neighbors noticed that she was selling far more butter than many other farmers' wives with much larger herds of cows. People began to look on her with suspicion, but nobody had proof of any improper activity on her part.

Sheila was a beautiful woman, and very soon a romance developed between her and a local farmer named Honest Bill. Most people thought that it would be only a matter of time before Bill married Sheila.

But exactly one year after their romance began, a young girl from the area returned to live at home, having spent three years in the United States. Bill's eyes wandered from Sheila, and within six months, he and the young girl, whose name was Emer, were married and settled down on one of the most productive farms in the area. Bill's sheep and cattle were the envy of many.

It is an understatement to say that Sheila Bawn was devastated by the breakup of her romance. Deep feelings of envy and jealousy toward Bill's wife threatened to consume her very being. She felt that she would never forgive Bill for the hurt he had caused her. Yet she managed to cloak her feelings and always acted friendly toward both of them when they met. They, in turn, responded to this friendliness. Soon Sheila began to visit Bill's house regularly, especially on churning day when Emer needed help making a large quantity of butter.

On one of these visits, as Sheila watched Emer energetically work the dasher up and down within the churn, a timber panel suddenly cracked and the rich creamy milk spilled all over the floor. Two weeks later, as the women were deep in conversation by the fire, six large plates from the top shelf of the cupboard came crashing down on the kitchen floor. Shortly after Sheila left the house, Bill arrived with the bad news that one of his best cows had drowned in the river.

No visits took place for three weeks because Sheila had to go to see relatives in another part of the county. During this time, Bill's house and farm were free of any misfortune.

As Sheila approached the house on her next visit, she noticed Bill plowing with his horse in a field close to the house. She waved as she passed and continued on to the kitchen, where she recounted all the details of her trip to Emer.

Suddenly a frantic shout interrupted their conversation and both women rushed outside. Bill was bent over the horse, which had obviously collapsed under the plough. Sheila offered to go for a local man who had the gift of curing animals.

"It's too late. The horse is dead," moaned Bill. "It's as if he was hit by a fairy stroke."

Five days later, a ragged traveling woman seeking alms called on Bill's house. She found the young couple almost in tears as they prepared for churning. In a very short while, they were pouring out their tale of misfortune to this total stranger. Suddenly she jumped up from her chair, removed her tattered cloak, rolled it up in a ball, and tossed it into the fire. Underneath she wore a beautiful red cloak with a bonnet, which she quickly pulled up over her head. She seemed to be a totally different woman.

"I know that you are surprised, perhaps even frightened, by this drastic change in me," she began. "Have no fear, and do not question who I am or where I came from. It is enough to know that I am drawn to places where there is evil." Bill and his wife were speechless as they stared at this strange woman, who told them that either a neighbor or a visitor to their house was working evil charms on them.

"It's strange, but when one of my closest friends, Sheila Bawn, visits us here, misfortune often strikes. But she has been the most helpful person in the whole parish, so it cannot be she," said Emer.

The woman in red did not reply, but turned her ear to the front door and then began to shudder. "Close that door quickly," she ordered, "for I feel evil approaching."

From her right-hand pocket, the woman took a fistful of withered herbs and tossed them in the fire. Almost immediately, clouds of smoke shot up the chimney. She quickly grabbed the poker and threw it into the fire. When it was red-hot, she used the tongs to pull it from the fire and traced the sign of the cross on the earthen floor.

At that very moment, a piercing shriek was heard from outside. When the door was opened, in rushed Sheila Bawn, screaming that a red-hot iron was burning its way through her body. She collapsed on the floor and her face turned black.

"There is the cause of all of your trouble," said the strange woman. "The sooner you get her out of here, the better. And have nothing further to do with her."

With that, the red-cloaked woman left the house and was never seen or heard of again. With the help of neighbors, Sheila Bawn was taken back to her own house, where she quickly recovered from her ordeal. But she was now labeled as an evil witch and shunned by all the people of the parish. Life became so miserable for her that she eventually left the area, and like the woman in red, neither trace nor tidings of her were heard again.

Bill and his wife prospered from that day forward, free from the evil influence of Sheila Bawn, and they and their children lived happily ever after.

A Famous Thief

Over the centuries, many tales have been told about Ireland's legendary thief, the Gadai Dubh. Although seanachies were always careful to point out that stealing was a despised activity, listeners to these tales always ended up with a certain degree of admiration for the tricks used by the Gadai Dubh to evade capture. In this tale, the Gadai Dubh's wits are put to the test when he challenges a young apprentice to out-think him for the reputation of the best thief in Ireland.

Of all of the famous thieves who lived in Ireland, few could match the skills of the Gadai Dubh. His daring exploits were talked about far beyond his native province of Munster, and he bore the signs of his lucrative trade. The Gadai Dubh lived in a fine mansion by the Lakes of Killarney, owned a large stock of cattle and sheep, and enjoyed all of the worldly comforts that money could buy. Whenever the tall, slender figure of the Gadai Dubh was seen approaching town, women would tighten the clasps of their handbags, bolt their doors, and send word to their menfolk to be on the lookout. Nothing was safe with him around. One old woman said that he would even steal the pepper off the Pope's soup! Time and again, he escaped from officers of the law, and he loved to boast that he was the best thief in Ireland.

About twenty miles from the Gadai Dubh's mansion, deep in the Kerry Hills, lived a couple with a fifteen-year-old son. The boy had broken their hearts, for he was lazy, mischievous, and disobedient. The only thing he seemed to be good at was stealing and thievery.

"What in the name of God are we going to do with him?" said his father to his mother one wintry night as they sat on either side of a blazing peat fire. "As far as I can see, the only thing that young devil is good for is stealing and robbing."

Gadai Dubh (*Gawd-thee Duv*)

"Well then, if that is the case," said the boy's mother, "why doesn't he make a career out of it? We could send him to the Gadai Dubh as an apprentice."

Then and there, the decision was made. The next morning at dawn, the boy's father mounted his horse and told his young son to jump up behind him. Soon they were heading for the mansion of the master thief. They couldn't have picked a better morning to come. The previous night, the Gadai Dubh had raided a wealthy man's house and had come home with one hundred gold, shining sovereigns, so he was in good form when he answered the knock on his door.

"And what, may I ask, brings you two to visit me at such an early hour of the morning?" he asked.

"I want you to take on this young fellow of mine as an apprentice thief," answered the boy's father.

The Gadai Dubh looked intently at the youngster and noticed that his devilish, shifty eyes never looked straight at you. His response was instant. "I'll take him on for six months and teach him every trick of the thieving trade. At the end of that time, I will set him three tasks. If he fails with any one of them, I will have to kill him, for I cannot have anybody reveal my secrets. If he is successful, he will stay in my service forevermore."

"I am willing to take a chance on that," said the father, "for he is not going to do any good at any other job. It might as well be you who kills him as anybody else, for I fear that is going to be his fate in any case."

It soon became obvious to the Gadai Dubh that he had taken on a very apt pupil. Long before the six months were up, the young thief had picked up most of his skills. Eventually, when the training period was over, he was called into a luxurious sitting room and given his first mission. The Gadai Dubh looked grave as he outlined the task. "Two miles from here, just beyond the crossroads, there is a tiny one-room thatched cottage in which an elderly couple live. It is their kitchen, their bedroom, and their sitting room. Tomorrow night, just as they do every other night, they will go to bed at midnight. I want you to go to the house after they have gone to sleep and steal the bottom sheet from under them. Bring it here to me before dawn breaks. I should warn you, I have told them to be on the lookout for an intruder. And remember, if you are not successful, it will cost you your life."

The master thief seemed to enjoy watching his smart apprentice shift his feet uneasily as the details of the task were unfolded. The youngster's mind would have to work overtime for the next twenty-four hours.

The next evening, as twilight gave way to darkness over the Lakes of Killarney, the young thief slung a shovel over his shoulder and headed for the graveyard. Earlier that day, he had heard that an old man had been buried in a grave just inside the gate. In the eerie darkness of the night, he began to dig the fresh grave until he got right down to the coffin. He unscrewed the lid and lifted out the corpse, and then slung it over his right shoulder. As he made his way toward the crossroads, he noticed that the little house still had a light on, but in a short while it was extinguished. He knew that the old couple would be asleep before long.

Finding a ladder in a shed near the house, he propped it up against the low roof. He then climbed to the top of the chimney with the corpse and dropped it down, legs first, into the fireplace of the one-room house. It landed not far from the bed of the old couple. The old man woke up, grabbed his gun, and fired a shot at what he thought was an intruder. To his horror, after lighting a candle, he discovered a dead man on the floor. A piercing scream from his wife echoed across the valley.

"We will be tried for murder. You'll be hanged and I'll be left a widow, alone here with nobody to protect me," she wailed and quickly blew out the candle to avoid drawing attention to the house. "Get that corpse out of here and bury it in the woods as fast as you can." Her husband promptly obeyed.

Lurking on the roof was the young thief. He allowed a good bit of time to elapse before easing in the door to the darkened house. Mimicking the old man's voice to perfection, he told the woman that he had dropped the body into a deep bog hole where it would never be found. As the young thief slipped into the bed beside her, supposedly shivering with the cold, she was convinced that her husband had returned.

"I'll die of the cold if I don't get heat soon. Your side of the bed is warm. Would you mind switching to my side?" requested the young thief. As soon as she got out of the bed, he wrapped the bottom sheet around himself, leaped from the bed, and scurried out the door into the darkness. Within a short time, he was back at the mansion of the Gadai Dubh, with the sheet!

"You have done well," said the Gadai Dubh grudgingly, barely concealing his amazement at the creativity of his young apprentice. "I want you here tomorrow evening to hear about your second test."

The second task involved stealing two horses from a farmer as he used them to plough a field in the early morning. The young thief was warned that the farmer carried a gun and had been alerted to the possibility of encountering a horse thief.

The young thief got little sleep on the night prior to this formidable task. He tossed and turned as he vainly searched his brain for a plan. Just before dawn broke, he rose and headed for the field. As he hid in a nearby grove of trees and waited for the farmer to arrive, he noticed a mother rabbit scurrying past and entering a burrow by the trunk of a tree. He darted after her, and reaching his long arm into the burrow, removed the mother and two other young rabbits, firmly holding on to all three.

He did not have to wait very long for the farmer to arrive with his two fine horses. As soon as they were yoked to the old iron plough, the farmer proceeded to open the first trench just inside the fence. As he began the second trench, the young thief released one of the little rabbits. It ran right across the path of the plough, in full view of the farmer.

"Ah! You little devil! When you grow up, you will eat the vegetables that I have planted in this field. I will put a stop to your gallop," he shouted as he drew his gun and fired. Luckily for the little rabbit, the farmer missed. As he prepared to fire again, the thief released the second little rabbit. Much to the disgust of the farmer, this one also escaped. By now the young thief had released the mother. The bewildered farmer focused all of his attention on the old rabbit. As it leaped the fence into the next field, he decided to pursue it.

Quick as a flash, the young thief rushed from his hiding place and unyoked the two horses from the plough. He jumped on the back of one and held the bridle of the other as he rode back to his master's mansion. If the Gadai Dubh had any doubts about the skills of his young apprentice, they were gone now. He even felt that his own reputation as Ireland's greatest thief was being severely challenged. The wily old master regretted that he had taken on this boy. He vowed to set him a task that would prove so difficult that it would cost him his life.

One night in late November, the young thief was called to the sitting room of his master, who eyed his young apprentice keenly before speaking. "Early tomorrow morning, I will leave for the market in the next town, where I will buy a black-faced mountain sheep. I will tie a rope around its strong horns and lead it along the main road all the way back to my mansion. Your task is to steal the sheep from me. As soon as I lay eyes on you, I will draw my gun. And I should warn you that I seldom miss."

The heart of the young thief was now pounding at an alarming rate, but he sat expressionless as he listened to words that could prove to be his death sentence. Outside, the wind howled in the mountain valleys. He felt like telling his master to shoot him then and there. This latest task was demanding the impossible.

A sleepless night followed as he sought some glimmer of inspiration that would spare his life. With no solution in sight, he decided to get out of bed and get to the market before it opened. As the sun rose over his hiding place in the alleyway of a back street, he watched the first stall-holder arrive in town. The craftsman set up a table on which he displayed an array of goods, including leather belts, watches, cheap toys, rainwear, and some shoes. From a box underneath the table, he removed a pair of high boots and placed them in the center of the table. They were made from the richest leather and had wonderfully intricate designs up the side. Suddenly an idea entered the head of the young thief.

As the stall-holder helped a man unload some sheep from a cart, the young thief swooped down on the stall like a hawk. Within a minute, he was back in his hideout with the expensive pair of boots safely tucked inside his overcoat.

Soon the bleating of sheep and the mooing of cows disturbed the peace of the sleepy town, as more and more people packed the narrow streets. Emerging from his hiding place, the young thief mingled with the crowds and kept a close eye out for his master. Within fifteen minutes, he spotted the Gadai Dubh making a deal with a farmer for a fine woolly sheep. Moving swiftly, the young thief scampered across the fields at the back of the town and arrived out on the main road. He rightly assumed that the old thief would be passing that way very shortly. He set down one of the boots he had stolen right in the center of the road and rushed ahead around a few sharp turns before setting down the second boot in a similar position. In a small wood at the side of the road, he climbed into a leafy tree that totally camouflaged him. From here, he could see for miles around.

As the Gadai Dubh made his way home with his sheep, he came across the beautiful boot. He picked it up, admired it, and felt its soft, top-quality leather. "A pair of those would suit me right well," he said to himself, "for I haven't seen their likes in all of my travels. But one is not of much use without its comrade." He pitched the boot over the fence and continued on his journey. Some minutes later, he couldn't believe his eyes when he saw the other boot on the road in front of him. "For once in my life, I failed to act when I should have. Why did I not pick up the first boot? I would now be wearing shoe leather fit for a king!" he mused to himself.

As he held the boot, there was a look of indecision on his face. The young thief, who had a full view, held his breath. He watched as the Gadai Dubh darted to the side of the road, tied his sheep to a tree, and quickly ran back to pick up the first boot. When he returned, his sheep was gone!

Ireland's most famous thief had been hoodwinked, and he was shattered. But rather than admit defeat, he rushed back to town and bought a second sheep. On his way back down the road, as he passed the spot where he had lost his first sheep, he heard the bleating of a sheep inside the wood.

"I know what happened," he said to himself as he listened to the sound. "The first sheep broke the rope and she is now loose in the wood." He tied the second sheep to the tree and followed the bleating sound into the wood. Little did he realize that it was the young thief who was imitating the bleating of a sheep to lure him away from the road. By the time he recognized his mistake, it was too late. When he got back to the road, the second sheep was gone! In utter disgust, he headed for home, only to find the young thief standing at his front door with a sheep in either hand.

What could the Gadai Dubh do? He walked up to the young thief and said, "Not only are you the best thief in Ireland, but there isn't a better thief than you in the whole universe."

From that day forward, a strong bond of friendship and trust developed between these two skilled thieves, who worked together for many years. As the Gadai Dubh got older, he cut back on his own thieving activities, but he continued to pass on his cleverness and his wits to a most competent apprentice.

OISIN IN THE LAND OF THE EVER YOUNG

Many Old Irish tales refer to Tir na nOg, or the Land of the Ever Young. This mystical land is said to be a place of great beauty with flat plains of lush green grass, purple mountains, glistening lakes, and bright gushing waterfalls. Here, nobody grows older than middle age and people never become ill. The people of the Land of the Ever Young are kind and loving, and anybody who sets foot here longs to stay forever. But as Oisin of the Fianna learns when he comes to live in Tir na nOg, even a place as wondrous as the Land of the Ever Young is not enough without friends and family.

For the warriors of the Fianna, one of the biggest events of the year was the annual deer hunt in Toomies Wood by the Lakes of Killarney. It was held each September, when the red-deer stags were at their best and would challenge the fiercest dogs of the most famous warriors. Nobody enjoyed the hunt more than Fionn's son, Oisin, who was the most handsome of all the Fianna. His courage knew no bounds, and he often risked life and limb in defense of his comrades. He loved his father's dog, Bran, and was seldom separated from him in his youth. Above all, he loved adventure, especially if it meant traveling to unknown territory.

On this sunny morning, Oisin led the hunt with Bran and Sceolan, who entered the wood from the east side. Within minutes, a noble stag was disturbed from his grazing. The sound of the bugles echoed in the hills, where they mingled with the excited shouts of the hunting party.

The fleet-footed stag led the hunters on a merry chase around Lough Leane and on to the hills near the Upper Lake. Bran had been fed the best food in preparation for this day, and Oisin was proud of the way he was gaining ground on his prey.

Oisin (*Uh-sheen*); Tir na nOg (*Tier neh Knowg*); Fianna (*Fee-ah-na*); Toomies (*Twoo-mees*); Fionn's (*Fewn's*); Sceolan (*Shk-gow-lan*)

With a mighty leap, the stag crossed a wide river in the Black Valley. Unable to make the same jump, Bran swam across, losing valuable time. Oisin, who was almost as fast on his feet as his dog, kept urging Bran on, but the stag disappeared through the Gap of Dunloe. "It's useless, Bran," said a disappointed Oisin. "He has beaten us." Bran cowered a little at his master's feet, but Oisin patted him gently and then sat on a rock to rest.

A sudden bark from Bran caused Oisin to look behind him. In the distance, he saw a white steed with a flowing mane approach from the top of a nearby hill. He couldn't make out who the rider was, but there was something strange about the way the horse seemed to glide over the rough mountain terrain. In an instant, Oisin saw a vision that took his breath away. There, in front of him, astride the magnificent horse, was one of the most beautiful women he had ever seen. Her slender body was clothed in the robes of a princess, and the delicate crown on her head was studded with shining jewels and diamonds that sparkled in the morning sun.

"Where have you come from, and how can I be of assistance to a maiden like you, whose radiance shames the wildflowers on this sunny morning?" asked Oisin, as he looked up at her in awe.

"I am Niamh of the Golden Hair, and I have come from Tir na nOg, where my father is king," she replied in the sweetest of tones.

"Pray, why do you grace the land of Ireland with your presence?" asked Oisin.

"I have sought you out, great warrior and poet of the Fianna, for your fame has spread to faraway places. In my land, people never grow old. There is no sickness, no death, no strife or discontent. We live in peace and harmony, and the sun never ceases to shine. I want to take you to this magical land, for you are the only man with whom I wish to spend my life." Her voice sounded like haunting music in his ears.

"I feel unworthy of your wonderful invitation, for you must have many suitors from the palaces of great kings and princes," Oisin responded.

Niamh (*Nee-ahv*)

47

"My parents have wished me to marry many times, but I wish for no man but you. Great fame and wealth await you in my land, and you will have my love forever," she said. Moving forward in the horse's saddle, she then asked Oisin to come with her.

He swiftly leaped up behind her and, faster than the wind, the horse headed through the Gap of Dunloe and on to Dingle Bay. As the steed approached the cliffs above the sea, Oisin became nervous. He seemed ready to jump from the horse's back at any moment.

"Have no fear, Oisin. This great horse of mine will gallop over the water as if it were dry land," Niamh assured him.

As the steed sped faster and faster on its way to Tir na nOg, strange, exciting lands, large expanses of ocean, snow-covered islands, and fiery mountains flashed before Oisin's eyes. Entering a huge wood, the horse finally slowed its pace and stopped at a small gatehouse shaped like a lantern. Two immaculately dressed guards opened the big iron gate and welcomed the riders. A fanfare of trumpets announced their arrival to the crowd of people waiting near the gleaming white palace just past the gate. A large group of young people surrounded the king and queen on the steps leading to the main door.

Oisin loved the warm welcome these people gave him and was astounded by the beauty of his surroundings. Not even the palace of the high king of Ireland at Tara could match this wonderful castle in Tir na nOg. Oisin greeted his new people, and they began preparations for the wedding. Within days, a wedding feast was prepared, and Niamh and Oisin were joined in marriage. The celebrations lasted three days and three nights.

Life with Niamh was beyond Oisin's wildest expectations. He was deeply in love and had riches in plenty. Worries and troubles never disturbed his happiness. One day he would be king of this wonderful land.

Oisin loved to stroll on the hillsides overlooking the wood that surrounded the castle. On one occasion, as he sat on a rock, he thought he heard the bugle sound of the Fianna calling the warriors to a hunt. He almost expected Bran to appear over the brow of the hill. Alas! It could only be his imagination. Suddenly he was seized by an overpowering longing to return to Ireland. He wished to see his father, Fionn, joke with his former comrades, and challenge Goll Mac Morna to a game of chess.

When Oisin returned from his walk, Niamh noticed that he was much quieter than usual. She knew that there was something on his mind, but it took her some time to discover the cause of his unease.

"This desire to pay a visit to Ireland and see my family and friends is consuming me. I must go," said Oisin earnestly.

"I have feared this moment ever since I married you," said Niamh anxiously. "But I well know that I must grant you your request."

"It would be the greatest gift you could give me," said Oisin, holding her hand. "And I will be back to you before you rightly know that I am gone."

Niamh looked at him gravely before she spoke. "I will give you my steed, but there is one solemn promise that you must make to me. You must not dismount from my horse, for if your feet touch the soil of Ireland, I will never see you again."

"That is something that I cannot live with," answered Oisin, as he clasped her hand more tightly.

Early the next morning, he mounted the white steed, bade farewell to Niamh, and with the speed of the wind soon arrived in his own land. His excitement heightened as he reached the Lakes of Killarney. He expected at any minute to hear the sounds of bugles, the baying of dogs, or the clanging of shields as the Fianna sharpened their fighting skills.

But all was quiet. He searched the caves that served as sleeping quarters on the slopes of Mangerton Mountain, but they were all abandoned and looked as

---

Goll Mac Morna (*Goul Mock Mor-na*)

if they hadn't been used for years. An old fisherman with a long grey beard was casting his line on the southern shore of Lough Leane as Oisin approached on his horse. "I was wondering if you noticed Fionn Mac Cumhail and some of the warriors of the Fianna pass this way lately," he inquired. The old man looked at him with searching eyes.

"Fionn Mac Cumhail and the warriors of the Fianna," repeated the old man. "Surely they haven't hunted this land since my great-grandfather was a boy. Tell me, have you been away with the Wee Folk all of these years?"

Turning his horse around, Oisin headed for the Fianna's winter quarters in the Hill of Allen in Kildare. But all he found were crumbling walls overgrown with ivy and nettles. As tears welled up in his eyes, he noticed three men in a field nearby. They were struggling to move a large stone toward a fence. They motioned to him that they needed help. As he neared them, he couldn't help but think how weak the men must be if the three of them together could not move the stone. Any one of the Fianna warriors could have thrown it half a mile away!

Oisin was just about to dismount and help the men when he thought of Niamh's warning. He leaned down from the saddle and, with his left hand, gave the stone such a heave that it rolled right to the fence. But the pressure on the leather saddle strap was too much and it snapped, sending Oisin tumbling to the ground. In an instant, the great warrior felt the life being sapped from his body. To the utter amazement of the three men, he was transformed into a withered old man. It was then that Oisin realized how long he had spent in Tir na nOg.

It must have been at least three hundred years. He knew now that he would never see his beautiful Niamh again.

As Oisin took his last breath, a loud whinny was heard from the white steed. Then it turned its head to the West and galloped home to Tir na nOg.

Lough Leane (*Lock Lane*); Fionn Mac Cumhail (*Fewn Mock Cool*)

JUST ONE CHOICE

The Giant's Causeway on the northern coast of Ireland has fascinated people for hundreds of years. It consists of 40,000 hexagonal columns of black rock, which form a raised roadway from the coast out under the sea. The Causeway is said to be inhabited by half-human seals capable of granting wishes. When Jackie O'Gorman encounters one such seal, he is reminded that making a decision for yourself is easy, but it becomes much harder when your decisions affect the ones you love.

Like their forefathers who had lived in County Antrim in the olden times, Jackie and Nancy O'Gorman were superstitious and had a healthy respect for the Wee Folk. The young couple lived with Jackie's parents in a comfortable farmhouse on a fertile thirty-acre farm overlooking the famous Giant's Causeway in the north of Ireland. Life was good. Jackie's father was old, but he was still able to help with many light tasks around the farmyard. His mother gladly watched her three granddaughters. Nancy found her help to be invaluable as she awaited the birth of her fourth child.

"If this child is a boy, there will be great rejoicing in our house," remarked Jackie's father, who longed to see a grandson before he died.

"If it's a boy, that cradle will have to be closely guarded, for the fairies are always looking for boys to fight in the fairy wars," said Jackie's mother. She knew that not long ago on nearby Rathlin Island, a healthy baby boy had been spirited away, and a miserable changeling had been left in his place.

On hearing this, Nancy winced. The idea of losing a child was unthinkable. Jackie loved his three daughters dearly, but it was his fondest wish to have a son who would grow up strong and healthy, help him with the farm work, and eventually take over the family farm just as he had taken it over from his father. Jackie had often dreamed of taking his son by the hand and looking out over the sea from the high field at the back of the farmhouse. There, he would tell him the story of the great warrior and giant, Fionn Mac Cumhail, who had built the Causeway down below so that he could walk to Scotland.

Each night before going to sleep, Jackie prayed for a son. Nancy's time for giving birth was fast approaching. "Surely it will be no more than two or three days," she confided to her husband one evening.

That night, Jackie had a strange dream. He found himself seated on a column of black rock down by the water on the Giant's Causeway. Suddenly a seal popped its head through the floating seaweed and looked him straight in the eye. "You are deeply longing for a male child, Jackie O'Gorman, and so is your

Fionn Mac Cumhail (*Fewn Mock Cool*)

53

father," the seal said. "Look around you. There are thousands of the six-sided columns of black rock like the one you are sitting on. Now look again closely. Between us is an eight-sided column. There is only one. Do you see that the top is shaped like a shallow bowl? Do you see that water collects there? If your wife drinks the water from its top, she will give birth to a boy."

When Jackie awoke the next morning, the vividness of the dream astonished him. It had seemed so real. He knew that he could pick out the very spot where the seal's head had popped up. He wondered if he should talk to Nancy about it, but finally he decided not to.

Unbeknownst to anybody in the household, Jackie approached the Causeway in the late afternoon of the day after the dream. The farm work was done. There had been some light rain and the whole area was shrouded in mist. To his utter amazement, he found an eight-sided column of black rock with some water lodged in its bowl-shaped top! Seal heads were bobbing up and down in the water just offshore.

Jackie realized his dilemma. He had always shared his secrets with his wife and family. Should he tell them about the dream? Would they laugh at him for having such a crazy imagination? Did Nancy really want a boy as much as he did? He remembered that she had been uneasy when she heard about the changeling on Rathlin Island. Then he had a thought. He could take a mug, scoop the water into it, and bring it home. But could he ask Nancy to drink it and not tell her or his parents? Surely, it could do no harm!

Jackie returned home for a mug, and then went back to the Causeway.

"Daddy, this is your second time going down to the Causeway today," said one of his daughters, as he approached the house again at twilight. Then she asked him what was in the mug.

"Just special water for a drink," he answered as he entered the empty kitchen.

"Daddy, may I see it, please?" she asked.

"Child, it is just water," he answered a little impatiently.

At that moment, Jackie heard his father shouting that two cows had broken down the gate leading into the potato patch. Placing the mug on the third shelf of the cupboard, he rushed out to save his potato crop. No sooner had he left the kitchen than his young, inquisitive daughter awkwardly reached up to the mug, accidentally knocking it over. Fearing her father's anger, she quickly filled the mug with spring water from a pail by the back door and put it back on the shelf.

That evening, Jackie shared the secret of his dream with Nancy. Both felt that there would be nothing wrong with drinking the water. Nancy carefully took the mug and drank it all.

The next day, Nancy gave birth to a baby girl. The disappointment at not having a boy was overshadowed by the beauty of the lovable new arrival. Jackie's mother ascended the stairs to get her first look at her fourth grandchild, but as soon as her eyes met the eyes of the baby, her power of speech suddenly left her. When she opened her mouth, no words of love or joy could be uttered!

Everybody thought that the excitement had momentarily overwhelmed her and that her speech would return shortly, but it was not to be. Weeks passed, months passed, and a year went by without any change. Her soothing voice and great stories were sorely missed. Her family, friends, and neighbors were deeply shocked. But there was still more tragedy awaiting the O'Gorman household.

After some time, it was discovered that the baby was unable to hear. It broke the hearts of her parents that their beautiful daughter would never hear their voices. She would never enjoy the singing of birds on a spring morning or be able to listen to her grandfather's great folktales of ancient Ireland. Jackie cursed the day he had taken the water from the Causeway and resolved that he would never be seen down there again.

But almost a year later, Jackie noticed that a number of logs from a wrecked ship had been tossed onto the Causeway rocks by the Atlantic waves. They would

make excellent beams for the small shed that he intended to build at the back of his house. Already a number of his neighbors had hauled up some of these heavy beams. Changing his mind about never visiting the Causeway again, Jackie ventured down in the early morning. As he struggled with a heavy beam, a seal's head bobbed up beside him.

"Don't you dare talk to me, you bristled old seal. You took my daughter's hearing and my mother's speech," he shouted. "You and your cursed water!"

Amazingly, the seal spoke. "That is where you are wrong, Jackie O'Gorman. Your wife never drank the water you took from here."

"Oh yes, she did," barked Jackie angrily. "I gave it to her with my own hands."

The seal continued. "This is no time for arguing. We have waited a long while for you to return to us. You and your family have suffered much, but this could be your deliverance. We will help you by giving you one wish . . . and one wish only. Go now. Talk to your wife and parents. I will be here to meet you at this time one week from today." And with that, the seal disappeared into the water.

At first neither Nancy nor his parents believed Jackie's story. But day by day, they began to notice that the pressures of life seemed to be weighing heavier and heavier on his shoulders. He had become unlike himself. He was quiet and was often impatient with his children.

Jackie understood his grief to be threefold. It saddened him to think that he would never have a son. At the same time, he could not accept his beautiful baby daughter's deafness. And tears often welled up in his eyes when he looked at his aged mother, who would never again speak.

When the four girls had gone to bed, Jackie once more pleaded with his wife and parents to believe his story. Finally, Nancy gave in. "If what you tell us is true, then go to the seashore tomorrow and wish that your daughter would get back her hearing. It's that simple."

Later, when Nancy had gone to bed, Jackie's father spoke. "You seem determined to go back to the Causeway tomorrow. If you do, wish that your mother would get back her power of speech. She is getting old and this affliction is slowly killing her. She has been a great wife and mother."

"But what about my innocent little daughter? She has a whole lifetime ahead of her!" came the sharp retort from Jackie. His father was silent.

Jackie, deeply troubled, knew that he would not sleep that night. He could make his one wish for a son, but that would be selfish. He ruled it out. His tossing and turning awakened his wife before dawn the next morning.

"Did you not sleep at all last night?" she asked.

"How could I sleep with such a cruel decision to be made before morning?" he replied.

"Are you out of your mind, Jackie O'Gorman? We have a daughter who is deaf and you have a chance to have her healed. I know you love your mother, but our child must come first."

As he walked down to the Causeway that morning, he rushed under a fairy thorn tree to take shelter from a sudden heavy shower of rain. A leaf fell from the upper branches and landed on top of his tattered cap, and Jackie remembered from old tales that the leaves of certain trees had supernatural powers. The leaf of the hazel tree was one, but he wasn't sure about the fairy thorn.

Gently taking the leaf between the fingers of his right hand, he removed his cap with his other hand and placed the leaf on his head. Then he replaced his cap. Finally the rain cleared and he continued his journey.

"I am glad that you believed and trusted me, Jackie O'Gorman," said the seal when he arrived at the water. "Now tell me, what is your one wish, which is certain to be granted."

As Jackie opened his mouth to answer, he felt as if he was not in control of his words. "I wish . . . that my deaf baby girl could hear my mother tell my son that she loves him."

"You have made an inspired wish, and it is my great pleasure to tell you that it has already been granted," said the seal joyfully. "Home with you now, where shouts of joy and peals of laughter will greet you."

It all came to pass, and there wasn't a happier family to be found along the coast of the Causeway.

PAYING THE RENT

Irish peasants have always had a great love of the land and were deeply resentful of having to pay high rents to selfish English landlords, who often had a very lavish way of life. Failure to pay rent meant that families could be driven from their homes onto the roadside while their thatched mud-walled hovels were leveled to the ground by a battering ram. For many families in the nineteenth century, the only thing that saved them from eviction was the arrival of money from America. In this story, Crohan O'Sullivan finds himself in a difficult position and learns just how important family and friends truly are.

Crohan O'Sullivan and his family had fallen on hard times, and hunger was stalking the household. As a child, he had heard his father talk about the Great Famine when the potato crop failed and thousands of people starved to death, but he thought that nothing like that tragedy could ever occur again.

As March approached, Crohan found that his supply of potatoes was running short. A blight had ruined half of his crop the previous June, and he had lost his best cow in October, when she fell from a cliff in the mountainous area behind his house. He had been forced to sell three other cows to make the rent for Mr. Bland, a cruel landlord who had threatened him with eviction. Crohan's wife, Mary, had few hens left, and eggs were very much in short supply. Soon the only meat available would be either hare or rabbit, and only when Crohan had a successful day's hunting. Mary sorely missed the extra money she earned from selling butter in the village, but all the milk their cow provided was now needed for the family.

As May Day came closer, Crohan knew that he wouldn't be able to pay the next lot of rent. Reluctantly, he was forced to contact his older brother who had

---

Crohan (*Crow-hawn*)

emigrated to New York ten years previously. He had never really been close to him, and except for a letter every couple of years, they had almost completely lost contact.

When the third week of April arrived with no response from America, Mary and Crohan began to panic. They could not bear to think about the prospect of being turned out on the roadside and watching as their thatched cottage was leveled with the dreaded battering ram.

One morning shortly after dawn, Crohan's dogs captured two rabbits in a wooded area about a mile from his house. The rabbits were a lucky find and would keep the household in meat for the coming week. But the trip to the woods served a dual purpose, because Crohan knew that he could find a good supply of hazel branches and twigs for making baskets at the eastern edge of the woods. Also from here, he was able to see the lower reaches of the mountainside and make sure his five young lambs had escaped the recent attacks of the one eagle that inhabited the area.

Crohan's work in the woods was interrupted by a call from the postman, who had just dismounted from his bicycle at the side of the road.

"A letter for you, Crohan," he shouted. "I'm leaving it on the stone since I have to hurry."

Within minutes Crohan was frantically opening the letter from his brother in New York. His eyes welled up with tears when he saw the crisp green one hundred dollar bill inside. It must have taken his brother a year to put this extra money together. Crohan's first instinct was to rush home to Mary with the fantastic news. Now they could pay the rent on May Day and there would even be money left over. A tinge of regret lessened his joy as he read his brother's short note—he wished they had stayed closer over the years.

When he got back to the edge of the woods, Crohan carefully folded over the envelope before picking up his tattered waistcoat, which lay beside the two dead rabbits on the ground. Turning the waistcoat inside out, he inserted the letter into a small hidden pocket and then put it back on the ground.

Overcoming his strong desire to rush home immediately, Crohan walked further up along the edge of the woods to cut some more twigs. He had just opened his penknife when he saw the giant eagle swoop low over where he was standing. In a blink of an eye, it landed on the spot where the two rabbits lay and grabbed one of them in its strong talons.

Crohan roared at the bird and dashed over to find the thief rising into the air, not only with a plump rabbit, but also with Crohan's waistcoat, which had somehow become entangled in its claws. His shouts of terror and anger echoed in the nearby valley as the eagle flew out of sight on its way to the hills.

As he trudged home, Crohan raged at himself for not putting the money in the pocket of his trousers. Many tears were shed that night around the O'Sullivan fireside as Crohan and his wife thought about the sad prospects for their family.

Soon word of the O'Sullivan's misfortune spread among their neighbors. It became the topic of conversation wherever people gathered. Father O'Shea, the parish priest, talked about it from the pulpit at Mass two days later and appealed to the congregation for help. This triggered an immediate response from a sheep farmer who lived in a remote mountain glen. He was hearing the story for the first time, and said that he had seen the eagle fly to its nest on a high cliff with a piece of clothing in its claws two days earlier. But he couldn't tell for sure from a distance whether or not it was a waistcoat.

Events now moved quickly, and later that afternoon several neighbors gathered with Crohan on the top of a steep cliff high up in Macgillycuddy's Reeks.

The sheep farmer pointed to a spot about two hundred feet beneath them where stunted blackthorn trees grew in a small cluster surrounded by clumps of ferns. He believed that the eagle had built its nest on a rocky ledge sheltered by the trees. Under the ledge was a sheer drop of another one hundred and fifty feet, making it a difficult location to reach.

Crohan suggested that with the help of a couple of ropes and a basket, a man could be lowered down to the ledge, but all agreed that it was a hazardous task. Not least was the danger of attack from the eagle at nesting time. And after all of the effort, would the waistcoat even be there?

Throwing caution to the wind and driven by desperation, Crohan sent a neighbor to his house for one of his own newly made baskets, three long lengths of rope, and a two-pronged pike.

On his return, the three ropes were firmly attached to the basket and Crohan climbed in, taking the pike in his hand. There was a sudden hush as the eagle emerged from the rock below and flew to the south, apparently oblivious to the activity on top of the cliff.

"A good omen," remarked one of the men, "but we must work quickly."

As soon as the bird was out of sight, Crohan was gradually lowered down along the face of the cliff. With his pike, he steered the basket toward the blackthorn trees and soon saw the huge nest, which contained seven large eggs.

"Stop!" he shouted to the men above.

His first instinct was to tear the nest apart with his pike and ensure that a new brood of eagles would never emerge from those eggs. But at that moment he spotted his waistcoat in a clump of ferns directly beneath the nest. He prayed that the money was still in the inside pocket.

"I see it!" he shouted hysterically to the men above. "Just slacken the rope a little."

Crohan was about to reach his pike into the clump of ferns and snag the waistcoat when there was a shout of panic from above.

"Look out! She's back."

Like a guided missile with massive black wings, the eagle was heading straight for Crohan. As he raised his pike to defend himself, Crohan saw the bulging eyes of the raging, panic-stricken bird. Luckily, he fended off the eagle's first attack, but now the bird was in a mad frenzy and intent on killing her victim. Crohan screamed in terror as the basket swayed erratically over the rock face and got jammed in the branches of the blackthorn tree. The men above were pulling with all of their might, but it was a useless effort.

Flapping its powerful wings with renewed intensity, the bird lunged at Crohan and tore a piece of flesh from his shoulder. As the blood trickled down his shirt, Crohan felt himself growing weaker. Mustering what strength he had left, he aimed a blow at the eagle and threw her back among the thorny branches of the blackthorn tree, where one of her wings became entangled. The powerful bird was partly immobilized and Crohan was within reach of his waistcoat. Was grabbing it worth the risk? What if the eagle got free again? Would Crohan try to kill the eagle with his pike?

With a swift jabbing movement, he pierced the waistcoat with one prong of his pike and retrieved it. Then he pried the basket out of the tree with his pike and shouted frantically up at the men to start pulling again.

"Faster," Crohan roared as he saw the eagle make a final effort to extract her wing from the thorny branches. Just as the basket reached the top of the cliff, the eagle broke free. She hovered ominously over the men. It was a warning and a threatening movement on the part of the giant bird, but everybody knew that there was no fear of attack, for Crohan no longer posed a danger to her.

Crohan's friends were shocked at his appearance. His head of black hair had gone completely grey. But there was triumph in his eyes. The one hundred dollar bill was still in his waistcoat pocket. A shout of joy rose from the top of the cliff, and two neighbors helped Crohan to the house of the sheep farmer, where his wound was washed.

It was not a serious injury, and later that evening a shaken but triumphant Crohan returned to his family waving the money.

From that day forward, Crohan and his family prospered, and never again had difficulty with paying rent to old Mr. Bland. Shortly afterward, the nest on the cliff face was abandoned, and the farmers of the area were nevermore troubled by the eagle.

Later that week, Crohan wrote back to his brother and thanked him warmly for his great generosity. He gave him a detailed account of his adventure with the eagle, and his brother responded with a letter that said he was fascinated by the story. It was the beginning of a new relationship between the brothers, and a regular exchange of letters over the years.

THE BOY AND THE POOKA

Stories of the Pooka spirit are well known throughout Ireland. The Pooka is a creature that often takes the form of a fearsome black dog or pony with fiery eyes. In other stories, it appears as a bull or goat. Although it can be nasty to those who upset it and may sound and seem frightening, the Pooka isn't really a dangerous or evil creature. When young Conor encounters the Pooka on a dark road, he learns that someone's appearance, no matter how scary it may be, doesn't always reflect who that creature is inside. And sometimes the things we are most frightened of are the very things that can save us from our problems.

There was a very good reason why the remote, mountainous valley in the hills overlooking Kenmare Bay was called Glenaphooka. As far back as the old people could remember, there had been sightings of a monstrous dog with shaggy, jet-black hair, a big head, fiery eyes, and a short stub of a tail tapering to a point. His favorite haunt seemed to be the stone bridge that spanned the Goleen River in the center of the valley, but local huntsmen had also seen him running along the upper reaches of the hills on Sunday afternoons. When lonesome, yowling sounds echoed in the hills, the people of Glenaphooka would remark, "Ah! The Black Pooka is at it again!"

"If you mind your own business and let the Black Pooka mind his, you need have absolutely no fear of him at all," advised old Jamesie, the valley seanachie.

His advice, however, failed to banish the fear from Glenaphooka. From an early age, unruly children were warned by their parents that the Black Pooka would take them away if they did not behave themselves. This threat caused generations of valley children to grow up with an uneasy fear of the otherworldly valley resident. Women and children were always accompanied by men if they

---

Glenaphooka (*Glen-ah-fook-kah*)

were out after dark. Even old Jamesie's son, Tom, a rugged, fearless, middle-aged farmer, had to admit that the hair on the back of his neck had stood up late one Halloween night when the Black Pooka had silently chaperoned him for a mile along the valley road before mysteriously disappearing into a clump of bushes.

Old Jamesie's grandson, Conor, loved to spend time in Glenaphooka. When an unexpected break from school came in early November, he couldn't wait to get to his grandfather's house. With him on board the steam engine was his new bicycle, which he would use to make the eight-mile journey from the train station to the valley.

Conor loved to ride about the valley roads and let local children admire his lovely bike. The young ones were thrilled when he gave them a ride on the carrier.

One day while his Uncle Tom was off helping a neighbor, Conor's grandmother mentioned that she urgently needed some groceries from the village store four miles away. Conor quickly volunteered to go to the store for her.

"Now, after you do your shopping, don't hang the bag on your handlebars. It could be quite heavy and might knock you off," warned his grandmother. "You have a fine carrier, so use it."

His grandmother also warned him not to delay, reminding him that winter evenings were short and that darkness came early. "Off with you now, my love, and God speed," she said as she waved goodbye to her favorite grandchild.

When he reached town, Conor parked his bike at the side of the store, turned the corner, and entered through the big glass door. It was unusually busy, but the wait gave him an opportunity to glance at a few comics on a cluttered shelf before the store owner, with a nod of recognition, asked him for his shopping list.

Conor's grandmother had been right about the weight of the groceries. The shopkeeper provided him with a sturdy bag and, with a smile at the boy, dropped in a free comic.

When Conor returned to the side of the store, his bike was gone! With a bewildered look, he scanned the street. Tears began to flow down his flushed cheeks.

"My bike is gone!" he screamed in alarm. Was that mocking laughter he heard in an alleyway down the street, or was his imagination playing tricks on him? Distraught, and hindered by the weight of his bag, Conor frantically searched alleyways without success. A kindly lady, recognizing his distress, suggested that he go to the police, which he then did. The policeman was sympathetic. He took down all of the details and promised to investigate the matter.

Twilight was approaching as Conor began the long walk home to the valley. He changed the grocery bag from hand to hand to gain some relief, but still he was often forced to stop and put it on the ground. Several times tears welled up in his eyes as he thought of the loss of his prized possession.

With some difficulty, Conor quickened his steps, as he turned off the main road to head up the gravel track into the valley. The light was beginning to fade, and he wondered if he would make it home before darkness completely enveloped the valley. Tall trees lined both sides of the valley road as it approached the stone bridge, and their high branches intertwined to form a dense canopy. The sound of Conor's footsteps on the rough gravel surface seemed to be much louder than usual as he entered the short, darkened stretch of roadway.

Suddenly he felt ice-cold, as if the temperature had dropped dramatically. Almost immediately there was a rustling sound in the bushes behind him. Not daring to look around, Conor began to walk faster as he struggled with his heavy bag. Just then he heard the soft patter of heavy feet behind him. Cold shivers coursed up and down his spine, and he felt as if he were about to scream.

Utterly terrified, he broke into a run. But the footsteps behind him kept pace. In his panic, he dropped his heavy bag in front of him, tripped over it, and fell headlong into a patch of grass at the side of the road. When he saw the dark, towering figure of a huge black dog looming over him, he became so paralyzed with fear that he couldn't even scream.

Conor knew it was the Black Pooka from the fiery glare of the two large eyes, like cinders of burning coal. He covered his own eyes with his hands lest he become blinded forever. Cowering in terror in the darkness, he felt sure that at any moment he would be devoured by this black monster, its white teeth gleaming like the blades of a huge saw.

Suddenly the sound of a galloping horse broke the silence. By now, everyone knew that Conor was missing. His Uncle Tom, having returned from helping his neighbor, was on his way into town to search for the boy. The sounds came nearer, but the Black Pooka did not move from the road.

Tom's horse crossed the stone bridge and gave an uneasy whinny. Suddenly it halted and tried to turn back. With great difficulty, and maintaining a powerful grip on the reins, Tom restrained the disturbed animal. A scream from the far side of the bridge tore through the night sky. Recognizing his nephew's voice, Tom dismounted in a flash and ran until he saw the side of the road illuminated by two balls of light. Seeing the screaming, cowering figure of Conor, Tom flew into a rage and flailed at the Black Pooka with his walking stick. But the stick met no resistance. It was as if Tom were swinging it through air. By now Conor had managed to stand up and was clinging to his uncle's coattail.

There was a hollow laugh from the Black Pooka and then it spoke: "Small need for you to be in a rage, Big Tom, so put your stick away."

The two were completely stunned. A talking dog! Nobody in the valley knew that the Black Pooka could talk. Their rage and fear miraculously melted away, and Tom's horse crossed the bridge and calmly walked up beside its owner. Conor became less tense. The moon appeared from behind Carrantuohill, Ireland's highest mountain.

"I have never harmed anybody in this valley, where I am condemned to wander in this sorry shape," said the Black Pooka. "Many times I have tried to help people, but they all run off in terror."

The Black Pooka told Tom and Conor that at one time, hundreds of years ago, he had lived as a rich farmer in the north of Ireland. Hundreds of cows in his area had died of a rare disease, and milk was extremely scarce. But being rich, he had a good supply. Late one night, just after he had retired to bed, he heard a loud knocking at his front door. It was a poor widow who urgently needed milk for her sick child. But he had been too lazy to get out of bed to help. Later he discovered that the child had died.

Carrantuohill (*Care-un-tool*)

"I died shortly after this incident and was condemned to live this life until such time as one person accepts my offer of help and thanks me," said the Black Pooka mournfully.

"There is little you can do for either Conor or me, Black Pooka," said Tom as he helped Conor get up on the horse.

"Except find my bike," whispered Conor, managing a faint smile, as his uncle mounted the horse behind him.

"I heard your cries, young man, and your bike may be closer than you think," said the Black Pooka, as he leaped over the fence into a clump of bushes, emerging with Conor's bike firmly clasped between his teeth.

All fear was now gone as Conor quickly dismounted from the horse and grabbed his bicycle. "A thousand thanks to you, Black Pooka. I will never forget your kindness," he said in utter delight. Then Conor and Tom watched as the Black Pooka crossed quickly to the other side of the road and glided through the bars of a farmer's gate as if it were a mere shadow.

That was the last sighting of the Black Pooka in that remote Kerry valley. Today women and children are no longer afraid to be out after dark, and Glenaphooka is a far happier place.

A Strange Night

Today, tales of adventure about Fianna warriors make up a large part of Irish storytelling tradition. Children who hear these stories can't wait to grow up just like their heroes. But what happens when three brave Fianna warriors encounter two woodland strangers who teach them a surprising lesson about the power of time? This story reminds us that youth should be cherished, and that there are things in this world that no one, not even the strongest warriors of the Fianna, can control.

Once there were three great warriors of the Fianna: Diarmaid, Conan, and Oscar. The men spent much of their time hunting around the Lakes of Killarney. One day an enchanted boar led them on a merry chase through the dense forest before finally disappearing into the remote glens near the top of Mangerton Mountain. The early onset of darkness that November evening made it difficult for the tired and hungry warriors to make their way home down the mountainside.

When at last they recognized the tall trees of the small yew woods by the Middle Lake, they knew they were on the right track. All they had to do now was follow the lakeshore to the camp, where there would be a tasty meal of salmon and wild herbs waiting for them.

At that moment, the three men stepped on a foidin seachrain, a tiny patch of earth on which the fairies had placed a magic charm. The charm caused people to lose their way, which the Wee Folk, who were usually hidden in a nearby thicket, loved to watch.

Suddenly the three warriors became disoriented. They went around and around in circles, vainly trying to find the lakeshore. At first they thought it a little amusing, but when Diarmaid heard a mocking laugh in the undergrowth, their amusement changed to anger.

Fianna (*Fee-an-ah*); Diarmaid (*Dear-mad*); foidin seachrain (*Fow-deen Shock-raw-ing*)

"You devilish pranksters of the night," Diarmaid shouted, "we will get revenge on you yet!"

It was close to midnight when Conan saw a light shining from a tiny cabin. "It is here that we will have to seek food and shelter, since my legs will carry me no farther," he said, as he approached the hut and knocked loudly on the door. After some shuffling inside, a withered old man drew back the bolt, opened the door, and welcomed each of them in by name.

"It is very strange that you should know our names when we have never laid eyes on you before," said Diarmaid, who looked at his host with great suspicion.

"Everybody who was ever born has laid eyes on me, as you will soon discover. But now come in and share what food we have, for you must be famished after traveling." Oscar looked uneasily at Conan, as they sat down around a fire.

Suddenly a door leading into a room at the rear of the kitchen opened, and a beautiful young girl with flowing hair and sparkling blue eyes appeared. The warriors of the Fianna had seen many lovely maidens in their travels, but none could match the beauty of the lady who now stood before them.

"Welcome Diarmaid, welcome Conan, and welcome Oscar, son of Oisin. We had almost given up hope of a visit from you this night." Her voice was like birdsong after a rain.

"Oh, beautiful maiden, you call all three of us by name, and yet our eyes have never before feasted on your beauty," Conan said. "I swear by the ancient gods of Ireland that there is something strange about this house we are in tonight."

Suddenly Conan heard a rumbling sound outside the back door, and the three warriors automatically put their hands on their swords.

The maiden moved closer to the three men. "Indeed all three of you have enjoyed my beauty for many years, as you will soon discover. But now, remove your

---

Oisin (*Uh-sheen*)

73

hands from your swords. You do not have to fear for your lives in this cabin. In a short while this table will be covered with food worthy of the guardians of Ireland."

The old man was falling asleep by the fire as the young girl brought out dishes of cooked venison, wild herbs, and honey from the room beneath the kitchen.

Halfway through the meal, the rumbling sound outside the back door grew louder. The door burst open and a wild mountain ram with curling horns ran straight for the table, knocking it over and sending the dishes hurtling to the floor. Conan, one of the strongest warriors of the Fianna, jumped up and tried to grab the ram by the horns. Within seconds he found himself flat on his back, the ram keeping him down with his front legs! Diarmaid and Oscar felt like laughing because Conan prided himself on his strength, but now the eyes of the ram were alternately beaming on them, as if challenging the men to step forward. Diarmaid lunged forward to grab the powerful horns, but the ram sent him flying to the far end of the kitchen.

Now Oscar joined the fray with the full intention of twisting the ram's neck and tossing him out the back door. But alas! He, too, met the same fate as Diarmaid. Just then Conan managed to free himself from beneath the ram's feet. He and his friends tried again to stop the ram, but all three of the enraged warriors with their combined strength could not contain the mad beast.

Slowly the old man rose from his chair by the fire, grabbed one of the ram's horns, and immediately quieted him. Then, to the utter disbelief of the warriors, he led the ram out the back door meek as a lamb. "It is now beyond the witching time of night, and for an old man like me and tired warriors like yourselves, it is time to sleep," the man said when he returned.

No words passed between the warriors, whose pride was sorely dented after the happenings of the night. In a short while, the old man was snoring in his chair by the fire. Soon Conan and Oscar began a troubled sleep on the floor by the wall, but Diarmaid remained awake.

He helped the maiden pick up plates and dishes, which were strewn all over the floor. He was becoming more entranced by her beauty with each minute. He told her that she was the most beautiful woman he had ever seen and that he wished to come back and meet her again when the Fianna were hunting in these parts.

"Diarmaid O'Duibhne, great warrior and poet of the Fianna, you and your friends will never again find yourselves in this place. Like many women throughout Ireland, I, too, admire you. But you had me once, and I'm sad to say, you will never have me again. Now it is time for you to join in the slumber of your friends." With that, she disappeared into the room from which she had emerged earlier that night and Diarmaid lay down to rest.

The old man was the first to wake when dawn broke the next morning. Diarmaid had to shake Oscar and Conan to rouse them from their slumber. All three pondered in silence the happenings of the previous night.

"Some things in life need an explanation," said the old man. "Listen well, warriors of the Fianna, I am Time. I age all things and I weaken all things. The ram is the world, which only Time can weaken and conquer. You saw me do that last night. The beautiful girl who served your meal last night is Youth. All of you had her once, but you will never have her again."

Then the old man led them outside and pointed to a small hill. "You will know how to get home as soon as you get to the top of that hill, but I ask you not to look back until you reach it." Then he bade them farewell.

A short time later, the men reached the top of the hill, but when they looked back there was no trace of the old man's cabin. And so, they descended the mountain with much to ponder and a strange story to relate.

O' Duibhne *(Oh Thee-nah)*

A Clever Leprechaun

The Irish fairy kingdom is made up of fairies who live in large communities and solitary fairies who are much happier living on their own. The best-known member of the Irish fairies, the leprechaun, belongs to the latter group and earns gold by making shoes for the Wee Folk. Although leprechauns are full of mischief and deceit, people love to hear about the clever ways they trick humans who are trying to steal their treasure. In this story, a salmon poacher who thinks that his frightening threats will scare an old leprechaun into handing over his gold discovers that wit is stronger than arrogance any day.

Brohgawn, the most famous shoemaker of all Irish leprechauns, lived in the fairy fort of Lissaree, not far from the present-day village of Sneem in the southwest of Ireland. This circular earthen fort was once home to a large troop of fairies, but was abandoned for a more scenic location by the Lakes of Killarney. Brohgawn, who had been the fairies' shoemaker for many years, had been granted Lissaree as payment, for there was a shortage of gold among the fairies at that time.

The clever old leprechaun loved his spacious underground chambers, including a secret room lined with thick metal that housed his pots of gold. Brohgawn had been very lucky in recent years and had earned a lot of gold fashioning shoes for the rich and famous in the fairy kingdom.

The leprechaun was very proud of the fact that he had made shoes for the royal household of Finnvarra, king of the Connaught fairies. Cliodhna, the fairy queen of Munster, had been so pleased with her shoes that she presented Brohgawn with a magic silver-handled knife. This priceless tool helped the leprechaun create shoes several times faster than any other shoemaker, for it cut each piece of leather exactly to size without the slightest waste.

Brohgawn (*Bro-gawn*); Finnvarra (*Finn-vah-rah*); Connaught (*Kon-acht*); Cliodhna (*Clee-u-nah*)

The other leprechauns were envious of Brohgawn's shoemaking ability and longed to learn some of his extraordinary skills. With one glance, Brohgawn could determine the exact size of a person's foot without taking a single measurement. None of his shoes ever took in water, and his magic knife produced the most decorative designs. Brohgawn also used the leaves and blossoms of wildflowers to produce exotic-colored dyes for his shoes. He was often asked to take on an apprentice, but each time he flatly refused for fear that the apprentice would reveal the secrets of his craft to the other leprechauns. Nobody was even allowed to enter his workshop. In fact, the key was always kept in a secret pocket inside his green jacket.

Brohgawn loved to work in the open air, but this was now becoming a dangerous practice for the prosperous leprechaun. Many people in the southwest of Ireland would have loved to get possession of the key to his workshop, and so he was forced to find secret places to work.

One sunny morning just after dawn, Brohgawn walked along the Blackwater River to his favorite haunt in a secluded spot among the tall reeds. He whistled merrily as he trimmed the soft leather on the top of the shoe with his magic knife. Without warning, he was suddenly grabbed from behind by an early morning salmon poacher who threatened to take him home and roast him alive if he did not hand over his pot of gold.

"My good man," said Brohgawn very calmly, "you do not have to go that far with me, for I will gladly give you gold aplenty. Hidden under a stone about a half mile upriver is a purse of gold, and if you do not have enough in that, I know where I can get more."

"My little man, I have to tell you that I do not believe a single word you say, and I'll not release my grip until the shining gold pieces are sparkling in the palm of my hand," insisted the irritated fisherman.

"Then let us make haste to the stone if you are so impatient, but I cannot leave my shoes and knife here unattended. Please allow me to bring them with me, for I have worked long and hard on this pair of shoes," pleaded Brohgawn.

"I'll not let you out of my grip for five seconds, you wily little trickster," replied the fisherman, as he firmly held the leprechaun in his right hand. "Leave your shoes and silver knife right there, and when you have given me the gold, I will gladly bring you back here."

"But they could be stolen by another leprechaun," said Brohgawn in mock alarm. "That knife is priceless to me. My livelihood is at risk. Why are you so cruel when I have promised you much?" Brohgawn knew that his secret spot was unlikely to be discovered by another leprechaun, but he hoped that the poacher would take some sympathy on him and let him go.

"Your promises carry no weight with me, for I have heard the old storytellers talk about your tricks. You will not stand on the ground again until I get your gold," repeated the fisherman sharply. "Now let us get going. You are wasting my day!"

"Please grant me one request before I give you your reward of gold. At least pick up my knife and hand it to me," begged Brohgawn, "and I promise you that there will be no further delay."

"You are a persistent little demon," blurted the fisherman impatiently. He bent down to pick up the knife in his left hand, all the while keeping a tight grip on the leprechaun in his right hand. As Brohgawn reached to take the knife from him, the fisherman looked at him intently.

"Not on your life will you get this knife until I get my gold."

"But you will promise to return it to me when I give you the gold?" said Brohgawn, hoping again to gain the poacher's sympathy. But it did not work.

"Less talk out of you from now on!" barked the fisherman in reply. "Come, let's go."

When they finally reached the spot where the gold was hidden, the fisherman was alarmed to see a big boulder instead of a stone.

"Did you lead me here on a fool's errand?" the fisherman yelled. "Who is going to move this boulder? If it cannot be moved and if I don't see gold within a few minutes, I'll take you home and roast you to a cinder on a blazing fire!"

"You have shot two questions at me and threatened me with death without giving me a chance to speak," moaned Brohgawn. "If you allow me to stand on the stone, I can quickly open a tiny crevice with one tap of the knife handle."

"No!" snapped the fisherman angrily. "You'll not touch that knife until I have my gold. I am losing patience."

"Well then you stand on the stone with me and I will show you the spot to tap," came the quick reply. Brohgawn was sure that the fisherman would not be able to stand on the slippery rock for long. When he lost his balance, the leprechaun would be free.

The fisherman, with Brohgawn still in his grip, climbed on to the large rock and Brohgawn pointed out a spot covered with green moss.

"One tap of the knife handle on that spot will open your treasure chest," said the leprechaun with enthusiasm. As the fisherman awkwardly turned the knife with the fingers of his left hand, a sudden anguished shriek tore through the morning air. The blade of the knife, like a poisoned arrow, had pierced the palm of the fisherman's hand, causing him to writhe in agony and fall headlong from the rock. His head bumped the trunk of an oak tree nearby, and the fisherman was temporarily stunned. The freed leprechaun extracted his knife from the victim's hand and ran off down the road.

Brohgawn was well out of sight by the time the hapless fisherman recovered his senses. "Such an adventure is not good for the heart," the leprechaun said to himself when he finally reached the safety of the fairy fort. "But it does make a good story."

And so, on festive occasions in Lissaree, Brohgawn amused himself and his guests by relating the tale of his clever escape. But his magical knife he kept hidden, vowing that never again would mortal or fairy look upon it.

THE LOST ISLAND
OF LONESOME SEALS

Hundreds of years ago, fishermen off the southwest coast of Kerry related stories of seeing lights from palaces and mansions gleaming under the water after midnight as they set their nets. Oftentimes they were so enchanted by haunting music echoing from the waves that they had to stop working until it ended. In this story, passed down by the monks of Skellig Michael, young Fiachra learns not only the source of the music, but also the importance of never disturbing a fairy fort.

In the dim and distant past, a group of people lived on a windswept, rocky island known today as "the Lost Island of Lonesome Seals." Life on the island was a constant battle against the ocean and the elements. The people survived on the eggs of seabirds, shellfish, and other fish from the ocean, as well as rabbits and hares. Potatoes could be successfully grown in only a few small fields.

It was well known that the Wee Folk from the Land under the Sea had an important summer residence in an earthen fort located right at the heart of the island. There were caverns and chambers hidden underneath the large, flat circle of ground, and strange, haunting music could be heard there on May Eve, on Halloween, and during the festive time of Lunasa. The fort was encircled by a deep ditch, with a high earthen embankment around the outside border. The area within was carpeted in rich green grass. The islanders knew that the Wee Folk wished to be left alone, but they had a hard time keeping their cows from grazing on the grassy meadow.

The inhabitants of the island had little contact with the mainland and were often totally cut off by stormy seas for months at a time. Once during a severe

---

Fiachra (*Fee-ach-ra*)

storm, the Lost Island of Lonesome Seals was isolated for most of February and March, after which there followed a terrible drought throughout the month of April. When the fishermen rowed their boats to the island cove one morning in early May, they were greeted by an astonishing scene.

May God preserve us all from harm! Neither the mooing of a cow, the barking of a dog, nor the sound of a human voice could be heard from one end of the island to the other. All human and animal life had vanished without a trace. The strangest thing of all was that this disappearance must have just occurred! Tiny wisps of smoke still rose from the chimneys of the thatched cottages, as dying embers of peat turned to ash. Unfinished meals lay on the kitchen tables, and farm implements stood in fields as if the workers were taking a rest.

The only sound the fishermen could hear was a loud wailing coming from the western coast of the island. They were familiar with the cry of the banshee, but this blood-curdling cry was different. Despite their fear, and thinking that some great tragedy had occurred, the fishermen crossed the island. From caves beneath the cliffs, dozens of seals were howling in unearthly unison. Something had deeply disturbed these creatures of the deep.

At first nobody believed the fishermen's story. But all of that changed as people visited the island and saw for themselves. Some would venture no farther than the tiny harbor, while the more adventurous moved inland. But they could find no clue that would explain the strange disappearance. There was no sign of struggle, violence, or death.

Various theories were put forward: The islanders had all been kidnapped by sea pirates. The freak storm had blown them all out to sea. Sea monsters had gobbled them up!

Then one Sunday afternoon, a holy monk from the monastic settlement at Skellig disembarked from his tiny boat. As he listened to the weird cries in the distance, he took a tiny bottle of holy water from inside his habit and sprinkled it on the earth. The crying of the seals stopped momentarily, but then started again with renewed vigor. Praying as he went, the monk quickened his step, crossed the rough terrain, and found himself approaching the grassy embankment of the fairy fort. What should he see when he got there but part of the green embankment dug away and the earth piled into the ditch. A plough had dug one trench in the circular part of the fort and was still embedded in the earth. Spades and shovels lay strewn around.

It took the monk from Skellig to discover that the islanders had interfered with a fort sacred to the Wee Folk. It must have angered them so much that they took deadly revenge.

Almost fifty years passed before anybody ventured near the island again. Who could ever get a night's sleep there with the constant, lonesome crying of the seals? The whole place became overgrown and the houses fell to ruin. According to fishermen, even the seabirds did not fly over the island.

Then one year when the fishing was very poor, a cruel chieftain took over the island of Valentia and evicted two families from their tiny farms because they were unable to pay the high rent he demanded. What's more, he told the people of Valentia that it would be a crime for anybody to give them shelter. Facing homelessness and starvation, the families packed their meager belongings into their boats, said a silent prayer at the holy well of St. Fionan, bade farewell to their friends and relatives, and sailed for the Lost Island of Lonesome Seals.

The Good Lord must have answered the prayers of these two unfortunate families, for they were granted fair weather for their voyage and within two weeks had made two ruined houses on the island quite habitable. The fishing around the island was good, and there was an abundance of shellfish and wild berries. Contrary to the stories they had heard, there were rabbits, hares, and foxes on the island. On the higher ground along the western coast, they found a small herd of wild goats. The taming of these wild inhabitants proved to be a formidable task, but without them they would have had no milk.

While all were very sad about leaving Valentia, young Fiachra Kearney, a freckle-faced ten-year-old, seemed to relish the prospect of a new adventure for himself and his family. He was the third son of one of the fishermen and was very different from any of the other children in Valentia. From his earliest years, he had spoken of playing with and talking to the fairy folk in the woods and around the rocks near his house. At first his parents took little notice of this childish chatter, but he spoke so naturally and convincingly about these elemental

---

Fiachra (*Fee-ach-rah*)

beings that they gradually became worried. To Fiachra's surprise, they discouraged him from talking about the fairy folk and warned him not to talk to other adults about his experiences. And so he kept his experiences to himself and became a little withdrawn.

Strange to relate, but when they reached the island, there was only one person who could hear the cry of the seals—Fiachra. He was not the least bit afraid of this cry, even when he heard it late at night. Many times he told his parents about it, but since neither they nor their neighbors had heard it, they dismissed his story as more of his foolish imagining.

Seals were very important to life on the island, especially when fish was scarce. Their meat had a fishy taste, but it was good to eat and, if salted, could be stored in a barrel or hung from the ceiling in strips. Seal oil was burned in lamps and painted onto the sails and woodwork of boats to make them waterproof. It also relieved pains in the bones. When butter was in short supply, people dipped their bread in the oil. The islanders even learned to make shoes from the cured skins of seals.

There was a strong tradition among fishermen that one should never be cruel to a seal or harass it in any way. But two incidents occurred, one of them involving Fiachra's father, which caused negative feelings toward the seal population at the western end of the island. Fiachra's father and his eldest son had been hauling in a net with a number of fine salmon wriggling inside when four seals managed to steal half of the catch. The men vowed vengeance on the animals, and some days later a number of seals were found dead in one of the caves.

The second incident involved a young fisherman who, in his effort to capture a seal, waded into the water of a cave when the tide was out. Suddenly he felt the powerful jaws and sharp teeth of a large seal grip his right leg. The seal didn't release its grip until the fisherman heard the bone in his leg crack. His heart-rending cries brought several of his neighbors to the seashore, including young Fiachra, who knew that there would now be another bloody slaughter of seals on the island beach.

On Sundays, men from both families met at the beach on the western part of the island and killed the seals. Fiachra was horrified when he saw the golden sands stained with blood, and appealed to his father to stop the killing. His father was taken aback by the intense manner of his son's pleading, but he did not stop.

Very late on one of these Sunday nights, Fiachra was suddenly awakened from his sleep by a lonesome cry that appeared to come from somewhere near his house. Prior to this, the seals' cry had always been faint and off in the distance, but this was different and frightening. It was so loud and intense that he expected to hear his parents get out of bed any minute. But nobody in the house moved. Leaping from his bed, he rushed into his parents' room, only to find them sound asleep.

"Get up quickly," he shouted in the darkness. "There is some trouble outside. Listen, just listen!" In an instant, his father had leaped from the bed, and then reached out for his son.

"I hear nothing, child. You have had a nightmare. There is no sound outside."

"There it is again, plain as day. You must hear it," insisted Fiachra.

For the remainder of the night, the young boy slept with his parents. No further mention of the incident was made the next morning. All the next day, Fiachra felt an overpowering urge to go to the seashore, but his father kept him very busy.

In the late afternoon, when he had finished his chores on the farm, his mother asked him to take a bucket and bring home a supply of fresh mussels from the rocks by the shore.

With a sense of anticipation, Fiachra carefully picked his way along the moist, slippery rocks to reach the spot where the dark blue mussels clung firmly to the base of the wave-battered cliff. Just as he began to pick the first mussel, he heard a splashing sound behind him. Turning around, he saw a seal emerge from the water. Then, before his disbelieving eyes, it shed its skin and a tall, slim young girl stepped out of it onto the sand. A seaweed tunic and skirt covered her body, and her toes and fingers were webbed. The girl of the sea bore a mournful look.

"I am glad you came to the seashore today, for you must know that your people are causing us much sorrow," she said in sad, measured tones. "Last week your people killed my father and uncle. We wish to make peace, and you are going to be the messenger."

"I am sad to hear that. You must know that it always grieved me to see a seal killed," Fiachra said with genuine sympathy. "But nobody will ever believe my story, not even my own parents. How can I be your messenger?"

"Our story is a strange one, but it must be told," she insisted. "You are the only one who can do it. You see, we once lived on this island just like your people. But we had a terrible drought that lasted for a full month and my people couldn't grow any crops. The land lost its green color and became dry and barren. Only one place remained green and fertile: the area around the fairy fort occupied by the Wee Folk of the Land under the Sea.

Fiachra remembered his father pointing out the rusted, abandoned plough and the old farming tools that still lay on that ancient site. "Were you the people who interfered with the fort?" he asked.

"To be sure we were, and we paid a dear price. Against the better judgment of our elders, we sought to sow crops on the site. No sooner had work begun than the Wee Folk became enraged and changed every human being on the island into a seal. You alone have been listening to our lonesome cries since you came to the island. As bad as our situation was before your people came, it is now much worse, for your people have slaughtered so many of us." Tears welled up in the strange girl's eyes and she stopped speaking.

"Excuse my tears," she continued, "but you are our last hope of ever gaining any happiness. Your people must repair the damage done to the fort. The Wee Folk have promised to reward your people and free us from our terrible grief as soon as the work is complete."

By now Fiachra was almost in tears himself and vowed that he would do anything to help. The girl asked him to listen very carefully as she spoke. "To help you convince your people, take a few of them with you to the abandoned house nearest the fort. The roof of it has caved in and only the front wall still stands. If you stand on the spot where the front door once hung and look overhead, you will see a large stone slab. Get one of the men to reach his hand into the small hole over the top of the slab. You will all be surprised at what he finds."

When Fiachra returned home, his parents scolded him for being away so long. His mother was particularly angry when he returned with an empty bucket, for he had completely forgotten to pick the mussels. "More chatting with the Wee Folk, I suppose," his father said scornfully.

"As a matter of fact, that is exactly what I was doing," said Fiachra sharply. "But this time I have some definite proof."

In a rush of words, he poured out the story of his encounter with the girl of the sea and begged of his father to come with him to the abandoned house. For the first time ever, his father seemed to listen as he looked at the pleading eyes of his son. "Perhaps this son of mine may have a sixth sense after all," he thought.

Fiachra's mother chided her husband and refused to go with them. Accompanied by two extremely skeptical neighbors, Fiachra and his father approached the abandoned house. Fiachra prayed that this was not a hoax. Then his father reached up over the stone slab and, to the utter surprise of all, found two gold coins! Fiachra danced with delight. Within a short span of time, all of the islanders knew of this strange happening, and almost all of them gathered in Fiachra's house. He was now a celebrity!

The work of repairing the fort began the very next day. The following night, for the first time since he had come to the island, Fiachra heard no crying from the seashore. For two full days, men and boys removed earth from the ditch and restored the embankment. The old rusty plough was removed and the circular area was properly leveled off.

This began a time of great prosperity for the islanders. Crops grew well and there was an abundance of fish. The seals were never interfered with again and Fiachra became their great protector.

Many years later, when Fiachra was approaching old age, the decision was made to return to the mainland. The cruel chieftain was now gone and better times were ahead. And so the Lost Island of Lonesome Seals was once more abandoned.

The island was not long deserted when the Wee Folk, who had long since forgiven the seals, took it down under the waves, where it still stands today. Now on this magical island under the sea, all live in peace, happiness, and harmony. And on May Eve and Midsummer Eve, huge banquets are held in the old restored fort, whose twinkling lights are seen by fishermen as they haul in their nets.

GLOSSARY

Amadawn (*Ah-math-down*)—A fool.

Banshee— A fairy woman whose lonesome crying at night is said to foretell death.

Battle of Gabhra (*Gow-hra*)—A battle fought on behalf of King Cairbreh in which the Fianna were defeated and then disbanded.

Blackthorn Stick—A common walking stick made from a branch of a blackthorn tree. Often used to defend oneself.

Bog—A stretch of fibrous, soft, spongy wetland that was formed over thousands of years from layer upon layer of decaying vegetation. Once dried, the turf from the bog was used for kindling in the hearths of Irish farmhouses.

Changeling—A fairy child that is left in place of one stolen from mortals. Changelings are bewitched to resemble the stolen babies, but have fiery eyes and puckered features, and scream continuously.

Charm Setter—A person who had the power to steal somebody's good fortune by means of incantations and rituals.

Codhladh Bealtaine (*Cull-ah Be-owl-tin-eh*)—From *codhladh*, the Gaelic word for "sleep," and *Bealtaine*, the Gaelic word for "the month of May." Also known as "May Day Sleep," a day when people stayed in bed late, for nobody wanted to be the first to light a fire. A charm setter could attract the smoke from the chimney of the first fire lit and take away all of the home's good luck for the year.

Cuchulainn (*Coo-kullin*)—Hound of Culann and the name given to the warrior hero formerly called Setanta, because he took the place of one of Culann's hounds in guarding his fort after he killed the animal. (*Cu* means "hound" in Gaelic.)

Fairy Stroke—Tiny fairy arrows that caused the human bodies they struck to wither and die. This allowed the Wee Folk to steal human children. The girls were needed in Fairyland as brides for fairy chieftains, and boys were needed to fight in the fairy wars.

Fairy Wars—Battles fought among the Wee Folk over land, forts, and other property.

Fairy Wind—A very strong whirlwind that starts without warning and is supposedly caused by the Wee Folk.

Fianna (*Fee-ah-na*)—A famous band of warriors in ancient Ireland. The Fianna was formed by King Cormac Mac Airt to protect his lands and was disbanded after the Battle of Gabhra.

Foidin Seachrain (*Fow-deen Shock-raw-ing*)—A piece of earth enchanted by the fairies to confuse humans.

Gadai Dubh (*Gawd-thee Duv*)—The Black Thief, said to be the best thief in all of Ireland.

Giant's Causeway—A group of 40,000 hexagonal columns of black rock that stretch under the sea off the northeastern coast of Ireland. The Causeway is said to have been built by the great Fianna warrior Fionn Mac Cumhail so that he could visit his girlfriend Staffa in Scotland.

Hail Mary—A part of the Catholic rosary prayer.

Hill of Allen—A low hill in County Kildare where the Fianna kept their winter quarters.

Hurling—A team game that is played with a wooden stick or bat and a small ball. Scores are won by striking the small ball, or *sliotar*, with a blow or puck of the hurling stick and driving it between the goalposts of the opposing team. Today, hurling is Ireland's national game and is extremely popular.

Lissaree—Where the fairy king dwells, from *Lios*, "an earthen fort surrounded by a ditch and an embankment," and *Ri*, the Gaelic word for "king."

Lough Leane (*Lock Lane*)—The largest of the Killarney Lakes in the southwest of Ireland.

Lunasa—The Gaelic word for "the month of August."

Macra (*Mock-rah*)—A group of young men, often sons of kings and nobles, who were being trained in the use of arms at the court of King Conor Mac Nessa.

May Day—A day full of superstition in ancient Ireland. Charm setters were particularly active on this day. It was well known that nobody should allow another person to remove anything from the house on that day because all of one's good fortune for the year might go with it.

Macgillycuddy's Reeks—A high mountain range in County Kerry.

Pooka—*Puca* in Gaelic, a shaggy, scary-looking dog, goat, or horse with fiery eyes. The Pooka plays tricks on people but never harms them.

Red Branch Knights—A group of warriors who fought under King Conor Mac Nessa of Ulster.

Rosary—A popular prayer of devotion to Mary, Mother of God, usually recited by Catholic families during the evening.

Saint Crohane (*Crow-hawn*)—A holy monk who lived in the Castlecove area of Kerry in the sixth century.

Salmon of Knowledge—Said to provide the first person who tasted it with the ability to see into the future.

Seanachie (*Shan-ock-kee*)—An Irish storyteller.

Slieve (*Shlee-ahv*) **Bloom**—A range of low mountains in Ireland's central plain.

Sovereigns—Gold coins used in England.

Staigue (*Shtay-ig*) **Fort**—A thick-walled stone fort that dates back to pre-Christian times and is visited annually by tourists. The Wee Folk were said to have a large feast at the fort on November Eve.

Straddle—A piece of equipment worn by a horse. It resembles a saddle, but there is a timber groove to hold a rope or chain across its center. When a horse is hitched to a cart, the chain that holds up the shafts of the cart rests on the straddle.

Tara Brooch—A famous brooch possibly dating back to the seventh century. It is made of gold and silver, and is exhibited today at the National Museum of Ireland. Its famous design has been copied for centuries and is common today in Irish craft shops.

Tara—The seat of the high kings of Ireland in County Meath. Cormac Mac Airt lived there.

Tir na nOg (*Tier neh Knowg*)—Also known as "the Land of the Ever Young," a magical land where nobody ever gets sick or old and trees bear fruit all year.

Wee Folk—Fairies

SOURCES

Back from the Fairies: Up until the early part of the twentieth century, many of the older folk in remote areas of Ireland believed that the fairies would steal away human children and replace them with changelings, or fairy children. Tales with this theme figured prominently in collections of stories by Lady Wilde and W. B. Yeats in the latter part of the nineteenth century.

The King with Horse's Ears: The story of King Labhraidh Loingseach is almost as popular as the leprechaun stories, and most Irish children come across it during the early years of elementary school. It dates back to pre-Christian times and was first recorded in Gaelic manuscripts written by the Irish monks in the seventh century. Today it forms an essential part of any collection of Irish stories for children.

Fionn Mac Cumhail and the Fianna of Ireland: Stories about the Fianna were very common in the oral tradition of my hometown of Sneem, because of its proximity to Killarney, where the legendary warriors hunted. Not far away is Lough Brin, named after Fionn's famous dog, Bran. Detailed stories of the Fianna appear in many folktale collections, including Irish Mythology, by Lady Augusta Gregory (2000).

The Greedy Barber: Daniel O'Connell, the famous Liberator, was a popular folk hero throughout all of Ireland, but stories about him were most common in the area where he lived on the Iveragh Peninsula. I first heard a version of this story close to Derrynane House, where O'Connell spent his vacation time. This tale and others can be found in Immortal Dan: Daniel O'Connell in Irish Folk Tradition, by Rionach Ui Ogain (1995).

The Charm Setter: As a child, I heard very few stories of this type, but as I grew older I was fascinated by the idea of how a person's good fortune could be taken away by an envious, evil-minded person. This story was inspired by a tale I heard many years ago from my mother, Margaret, coupled with Kevin Danaher's informative book of folklore, The Year in Ireland (2001).

A Famous Thief: This was my grandfather's favorite story, and I was fascinated by it for the first time at the age of seven. I remember asking him to repeat it on several occasions, and I even reprimanded him once for omitting a certain detail! This popular story had been handed down for generations in the area where I am from, and I have recorded it here with very few changes.

Oisin in the Land of the Ever Young: Stories about Oisin and his time in Tir na nOg have been passed down in Irish families from generation to generation. This story can also be found in Irish Mythology (2000) by Lady Augusta Gregory.

Just One Choice: Many fairy tales and some folktales involve the granting of wishes. If you make a mistake with either your first or second wish in these stories, there is still time to redeem yourself with the third wish. If, however, you have only one choice and you have three pressing needs, what should you do? In my story, Jackie O'Gorman was faced with that dilemma, and I had to think of a way out for him. I found the answer in the summer of 2006, when I paid one of my many visits to the Giant's Causeway and watched the seals bob their heads up and down in the ocean beside the black rocks. Other tales about the causeway can be found in Finn MacCoul and His Fearless Wife: A Giant of a Tale from Ireland *by Robert Byrd (1999) and* Fionn and the Scottish Giant: Ancient Irish Legends *by Padraic O'Farrell (1995).*

Paying the Rent: *As a child, I knew people whose parents were evicted by English landlords for not paying their rent. Many of my own relatives emigrated to the United States and sent home money to help out their parents. These two facts, together with a story I once heard from Tady Pad O'Sullivan, provided the inspiration for this story of Crohan O'Sullivan's encounter with the eagle.*

The Boy and the Pooka: *Although my grandfather assured me that the Pooka was harmless, his vivid description of this hairy being convinced me that I never wanted to meet him! This story is based on the question, "What if I had met him on a winter evening after I had gotten my first bicycle at the age of ten?" Other first-hand accounts of people's encounters with the Pooka can be found in* The Middle Kingdom *(1960) by D. A. McManus.*

A Strange Night: *To find out more about the foidin seachrain, read* The Middle Kingdom *by D. A. McManus. Many tales of the warriors mentioned in this story can be read in* Irish Mythology *(2000) by Lady Augusta Gregory.*

A Clever Leprechaun: *Stories of how leprechauns outwit humans are part of all Irish story anthologies. This story, which cannot be found in any anthology, was inspired by a tale my grandfather told me as we both walked through the fairy fort of Lissaree more than fifty years ago.*

The Lost Island of Lonesome Seals: *As a child, I heard many stories of fishermen who had strange experiences at sea late at night as they prepared to haul their nets. There is even an old belief in West Clare that the submerged village of Kilstephen lies at the bottom of Liscannor Bay and that fishermen can see its lights on certain nights. A similar story entitled "The Enchanted Island" can be found in* Irish Wonders *by D. R. McAnally Jr. (1996).*